The Apostle

A Screenplay by Robert Duvall

BOULEVARD BOOKS, NEW YORK

OCTOBER
BOOKS

OCTOBER BOOKS, NEW YORK

THE APOSTLE

An October/Boulevard Book / published by arrangement with
October Films, Inc.

Photos: Van Redin

PRINTING HISTORY
October/Boulevard trade paperback edition / March 1998

The October Books World Wide Web site address is
http://www.octoberfilms.com

The Penguin Putnam Inc. World Wide Web site address is
http://www.penguinputnam.com

ISBN: 0-425-16607-4

PRINTED IN THE UNITED STATES OF AMERICA

10   9   8   7   6   5   4   3   2   1

Introduction

Years ago, when I was returning to the East Coast from California, I decided to deplane in Memphis and grab a Trailways bus back west again for about thirty miles. My destination was Hughes, Arkansas. I was about to begin rehearsals for a new off-Broadway play and the character I was to portray was from this small town in the low, hot flatlands of eastern Arkansas. So a gathering of facts for a better portrayal seemed in line. The play was a new and fresh piece by William Snyder entitled *The Days & Nights of Beebee Fenstermaker*. When I arrived in Hughes, there wasn't much of anyone or anything there to greet me, so I wandered around a bit until I found a place to sleep since there were no hotels or motels. A group of road workers from northern Louisiana let me bunk in with them, and from the beginning to the end of my short visit they could not comprehend why I would stop on a flight from Hollywood to New York City to spend a night in Hughes.

They were most cordial and friendly, while the sheriff gave me nothing but strange and hostile looks, as perhaps he well should have. The town consisted of about ten or twelve stores, most all of these stores were owned and run by Chinese people. There were, I'm sure, any number of churches in this small town, as there always are in the South, but I was aware only of one very close to where I was staying. And since there was probably nothing much else to do there, I walked into my first Holiness or Pentecostal Church service.

It was most memorable. The main preacher was a round, plump lady who spoke openly and directly to her congregation. Her accent was thick and regional, and certainly pleasant to my ears. A guest preacher sang and played an acoustic guitar. He then began to preach in that rhythmic cadence that comes so naturally to these particular Christian people. And I suppose it is this one element, this style of preaching, that has stayed with me through the years and perhaps was one of the main reasons I wanted some day to play one of these Holy Ghost preachers. I knew from that moment on, this was something I had to do in my career as an actor—to portray one of these men whose preaching style has been called one of the few truly American art forms. I visited a multitude of churches throughout the United States, but this small, intimate church will always be fixed in my memories.

I developed my own script dealing with this particular subject. It took a number of fruitful years for my ongoing research to reach its fulfillment. The blessings and rewards of such a venture would be difficult to explain to others or even to myself. I finished the script thirteen years ago. It took me about six weeks to write. Rewrites and adjustments went on right up to and during the filming process. There was not a nickel to be found in Los Angeles, New York City or anywhere else that I know of.

A year and a half ago, my CPA, Joel Jacobson, said that I was in a financially safe enough position to finance the film. I knew him to be a conservative and honest person, so I figured if he said, "Let's go"—out of the blue—then it was time. It was he who "green-lit" the picture.

I had put everything on the back burner—gladly—because I was more than a bit apprehensive about the whole project. However, the pre-production went smoothly as did the actual filming. Rob Carliner, our producer, put together a wonderful crew that worked smoothly and efficiently. We finished filming a day early and took our time editing at my farm in Virginia.

This subject matter, and the world around it, has so often been caricatured in the past, and this is something I carefully tried to avoid. I think we have put forth a valid statement. In script form, concepts can be clean and yet cerebral. It is then up to the filmmaker to transfer the ink to behavior, and that is always the most exciting part for me. From ink to behavior.

The film is finished, and as I have always felt, one that had to be done. I believe the trip from the cradle to the grave is unique and distinct for each and every one of us. Certainly my journey has been enriched with the making and the completion of this film.

Foreword

Robert Duvall, as an actor, has always had a remarkable sense of American life, never dealing in clichés or in any way sentimentalizing this life.

Now here in *The Apostle*, as a writer, director, and actor, he brings all the knowledge he has acquired through the years to a wondrous culmination. The film is brilliantly written and directed by him, and his performance as The Apostle is in all ways remarkable.

—Horton Foote
November 1997

EXT. HIGHWAY—DAY

SONNY driving along a highway with his MOTHER seated by him. As he is driving, he notices about a quarter of a mile in front of him cars and people gathered on the sides and also near the middle of the road. As he approaches, he sees that a very serious accident has occurred. There are about two or three automobiles involved. The police are there, but no ambulance has arrived as yet. One car is jammed down into a ditch while the other two cars are upright, but dented quite badly. He decides to stop, and gets out to see where things stand and to see if he can possibly be of any assistance.

He heads for the car that is jammed in a ditch, knowing that he will have to encounter the Texas STATE TROOPER that is keeping people away. He slips behind the trooper and walks directly to the scene of the accident.

EXT. EMBANKMENT—DAY

As soon as the Officer's back is to him, Sonny walks down the little embankment to the crushed car and peers through the open window. Inside he sees a YOUNG MAN behind the wheel. He is sitting straight up, not necessarily out of choice, since the steering wheel is jammed into his chest.

A YOUNG WOMAN, in her early twenties, possibly his wife, is jackknifed over with her head near her husband's right knee, as if she had tried to hold on to him or grab for him at the moment of impact.

The young man's eyes are open and he seems in deep shock. The woman appears possibly to be dead or certainly unconscious. There is blood on the seat and floor where the young woman is, although it isn't apparent as to where it's coming from. There is an occasional distant sound that seems to come from the back of the young man's throat. It is very still. Sonny has to kind of stoop down in order to get his head into the window to get a better look. He manages to twist his shoulder and cock his head in such a way that when his upper body is put through the window, his face is facing the young man's at a rather tilted angle. Once he manages to do this, he is able to survey the situation in a firsthand manner, although it is a rather uncomfortable position and quite cramped.

SONNY: Son, can you hear me? You don't have to say anything. Just know that I'm a minister of the Lord and I want you to know that the Lord loves you here today. And I love you. If you can't answer, just nod and if you can't nod, just think it. Answer me in your mind and in your heart.

Sonny reaches in and puts the hand of the man on the woman's arm. The man's hand seems as if it had been intending to do just that, but had fallen short. He then puts his hand on the man's shoulder.

SONNY *(continuing):* If the Lord were to call you right now, would you be ready?

CUT TO:

YOUNG MAN:

Just looking straight ahead—or possibly a TWO SHOT would be better throughout the entire scene. We don't know if he is with Sonny or not.

SONNY: Do you accept the Lord Jesus Christ as your personal Saviour? Are you ready for him? . . . *(pause)* Are you ready to follow him and accept him at this very instant?

CLOSE ON—young man's face in shock but listening.

BACK TO SCENE.

SONNY *(continuing):* If you open your heart and let him come in, then he will stand with you whether you go home or whether you stay here with us. If you are called on home, will you be ready, because he's ready. And if it isn't your time, he will stand by you, brother, both you and your wife. He'll deliver you through this entire ordeal. There are angels even in this automobile at this precise moment. Even at this moment, he has sent his angels to watch over you. Do you accept him here today? *(pause)*

CLOSE ON—*young man.*

It's not totally clear, but it appears that he is thinking an affirmative nod.

CUT TO:

EXT. OF CAR

As one of the State Troopers taps Sonny on his leg.

OFFICER: Mister, you'll have to get out of there. You can't be in there. Let's go, get out!

We can SEE Sonny's leg kick out at the cop as if there were a dog nipping at him. It's a clumsy ordeal that we see and certainly strangely comical.

BACK TO:

INT. CAR

Sonny is talking. He is very, very concentrated and is trying to connect with the young man, and also his wife, as clearly as possible.

SONNY: Now, when that ambulance gets you, and you're on your way, you're gonna fly down that highway.

The Lord's gonna have a whole flock of his angels lead you on down that highway, you hear me? He's gonna go all the way with you. You've taken the Lord today and he's gonna go all the way with you. You both are his champions here today. Praise God!

CUT TO: Young man barely saying "Thank you, sir."

BACK TO SCENE.

SONNY: Don't have to thank me, son, thank our Lord and Savior Jesus Christ. You're in his hands now. Bless you both.

He exits.

EXT. CAR

Sonny backs himself out of the squashed-up position he's in and stands up in the open once again.

OFFICER: You can't be here. Now just go back to your car. You're not allowed here.

SONNY: Yes, sir, thank you very much, Officer.

The two are a bit testy with each other.

OFFICER: You really think you accomplished something in there?

SONNY: I know I did.

OFFICER: What?

SONNY: All I know is that I did not put my head through the window in vain.

OFFICER: How would you know that?

SONNY: When two or more are gathered in my name there will I be also. *(quoting the scripture . . .)*

OFFICER: Is that right.

SONNY: Yes, sir.

Sonny goes and gets in his car.

He eases into the one passing lane and proceeds on as the State Trooper's gaze follows him.

As Sonny and his mother proceed down the highway, we hear strains of "Ain't No Grave Gonna Hold My Body Down" faintly over the radio. We go back in time to an old radio station.

INT. SMALL COUNTRY CHURCH (1930s)—DAY

FIVE-YEAR-OLD SONNY with BLACK NANNY going into a country church to witness BLACK PREACHER in front of an all-Black congregation of 15–20 people.

CREDITS ROLL.

INT. MRS. DEWEY SR.'S LIVING ROOM—DAY

Sonny playing the piano with his nine-year-old DAUGHTER playing the right hand, while his ten-year-old SON stands to their right, as all three sing the same song that young Sonny was singing in the scene just prior to this.

Sonny's wife, JESSIE, is revealed during the course of the scene standing off to the side, quietly observing the little trio singing to MRS. DEWEY SR., who is sitting in either a chair or on a daybed. As they finish their informal little singing recitation, Mrs. Dewey Sr. applauds and says:

MRS. DEWEY SR.:   Oh, that's so nice, Sonny. Thank you, little children.

SONNY: When vacation Bible school is over, we're going to try to sing a little together at the Temple. *(as he kisses daughter)* Maybe Momma'll play the organ for us, if we ask her to. *(looks at his wife)*

MRS. DEWEY SR.:   I'll be there. Be sure to let me know when it's gonna be, you hear?

JESSIE: We'd better go on now and let Grandmother rest. *(looks toward her husband)*

SONNY: Give Grandma a big old hug and a kiss. *(he has to give his son a gentle shove)* Come on, honey.

MRS. DEWEY SR.:   I never see you and you're rushing off. Why don't you stay a little while?

Both children are hugging their grandmother. Sonny and Jessie glance at each other. Sonny smiles almost politely at his wife. There is a slight suggestion of tension between them.

SONNY *(to his wife)*:   Do you want to play for us, Momma?

JESSIE: We'll see. Bobby and Jess, let's go now.

Sonny goes to his mother.

SONNY: I'll call you.

MRS. DEWEY SR.:   When will you be back?

SONNY: In a little less than a month. About three weeks. I love you and the Lord loves you. You take care. *(he tucks a blanket around her)*

Jessie and the children head out the front door while Sonny is several steps behind them.

MRS. DEWEY SR.:   Sonny, could you get my other comforter? I'm a little chilly.

SONNY: You all right?

MRS. DEWEY SR.:   Yes, just get me my blanket, I feel I need it.

She appears a little weak-looking all of a sudden. Sonny heads for the back bedroom.

INT. BACK BEDROOM—DAY

Sonny comes in and gets the comforter; he notices a picture of him and his brother, ROBBIE. He looks at it for a short while, quite intently, and then goes to take the comforter to his mother. He hears her say "Sonny" and he answers:

SONNY: I'll be right there.

INT. LIVING ROOM—DAY

When he returns, he is a slight bit taken aback when he finds his mother lying on her back with her feet a bit up in the air and her eyes closed. She is on the floor. He looks at her for a moment and says:

SONNY: Momma, listen to me, I'm not gonna take you with me, okay? So just get on back in your chair. You hear me?

Sonny pauses. There is no answer. Sonny starts for the door; as he does, he stops before he goes out.

SONNY *(continuing):*   All right, I know you've died on me and gone on home to Heaven so I hope you can still hear me. *(he smiles)* I'll be back in less than three weeks, so you be good while I'm gone and I'll call you tonight. *(looks at her for a moment and then, as he leaves:)* I can't take you with me now.

After the door closes, the CAMERA COMES IN a bit closer on Mrs. Dewey. She opens one eye and looks after Sonny, as we . . .

CUT TO:

EXT. MRS. DEWEY SR.'S HOUSE—DAY

CAMERA BRINGS Sonny out of his mother's front door. He jogs over to Jessie's car. HORACE, the youth minister, is about to get into the car with Jessie and

*the children. Sonny goes to the back window and
kisses his kids good-bye.*

SONNY: I'll call you, Jessie, to see if you want to fly up to
Little Rock and drive back with me and Joe.

JESSIE: We'll see. I've got my Woman's Aglow meeting,
but call me anyway.

SONNY: Right. See you in a few weeks. Horace, bless you.

HORACE: Bye, Sonny, have a safe trip.

SONNY: I'll do my best.

*Jessie starts the car and eases on out into the street.
Sonny tells the kids to make sure they learn the
books of the Bible. They say, "Let's hear you." As they
drive away, Sonny rattles off books from the Bible.*

*The kids wave good-bye and yell after their daddy.
As he waves back, Sonny walks to his car and gets
in. As he starts the motor, he reflects oddly for a short
moment. As the car pulls out, we . . .*

CUT TO:

INT. TENT MEETING—DAY

*Camera reveals Sonny, along with his friend JOE
preaching with five other preachers. Here, we witness
a form of tag-team preaching.*

INT. LARGE ROOM—NIGHT

Sonny preaches to a small AUDIENCE of about

twenty or thirty Latinos alongside a MAN who simultaneously translates his words into Spanish. Joe watches from the side.

INT. SMALL, EMPTY CHURCH—NIGHT

CAMERA REVEALS a rehearsal of a religious trio— Joe, along with TWO OTHERS, singing a beautiful hymn ("Because He Lives"). CAMERA HOLDS on the singing and then PANS DOWN hallway to:

Two black cleaning LADIES opening a door in the back of a church in order to tidy up the office.

INT. ANOTHER ROOM—NIGHT

When the door is opened, Sonny is revealed sitting, facing a PRETTY BLACK WOMAN. Their legs are draped loosely over each other's. Sonny turns to the two cleaning ladies and snaps:

SONNY: Can't you see I'm administering to this woman? Please shut the door?

As the women close the door, one says to the other:

WOMAN: I guess he's administering to her, if that's what he says he's doing.

As they walk down the hallway.

OTHER WOMAN: Once you go black, you never go back!

CUT TO:

INT. SMALL CHURCH—NIGHT

Sonny has an ELDERLY LADY walking away from her wheelchair. He goes and gets her wheelchair, sits in it and wheels it to where she is creeping along:

SONNY: Now you give me a little ride here—you push me. I want to make the Devil mad, you hear me?

The audience, including Joe, applauds with warm enthusiasm.

SONNY *(continuing)*: Let's give a love wave to the Lord on high . . .

As they all begin to sing we

CUT TO:

INT. LARGE CIVIC AUDITORIUM—DAY

As Sonny preaches, camera reveals a largely ALL-BLACK MALE AUDIENCE. After each question that Sonny asks, such as "Who is our Saviour? Where does our power lie? And, who is our Alpha and Omega?", the largely all-black male audience replies with raised clench fists . . . "Jesus!"

EXT. SMALL MOTEL—NIGHT

Sonny's car approaches the motel as Joe and Sonny finish talking about the brother Sonny hardly hears from. The car pulls up to the motel rooms, the two men say good night and go into their separate rooms.

INT. MOTEL ROOM—NIGHT

We fade up on Sonny in a deep sleep. This prior action should have the voiceover of Sonny's prayers before he goes to sleep. The V.O. ends as we SEE him sleeping.

SONNY *(V.O.):* Dear Lord, bless Robbie tonight that he may someday accept Jesus Christ as his savior, oh Lord, bless and look over my two beauties, Bobby and little Jess, look over my beautiful wife and my beloved mother in the name of Jesus Christ of Nazareth. I thank thee Lord for all the blessings that you have so graciously given me in Jesus' name. Amen.

As V.O. has ended, we HOLD ON the sleeping figure of Sonny for a short spell. All of a sudden, Sonny sits straight up in bed. What he has seen in his dream is clear to him: He knows it to be the truth, God has opened his eyes! He gets up, dresses quickly, pounds on the wall, and yells to Joe, "Get dressed, it's time to leave." Sonny leaves the motel and heads back for the Dallas/Fort Worth area, to his home.

EXT. HIGHWAY—NIGHT

Sonny speeds that three hundred miles as quickly as he can.

SONNY: I can inform God of nothing, He knows all.

CUT TO:

EXT. DEWEY TRAILER HOME—DAY

Sonny arrives at his house—which is a very large mobile home—his wife's car is not there.

INT. DEWEY TRAILER HOME—DAY

He goes inside. The bed is made—a frightening sight. He goes to a dresser drawer and takes a .38 pistol out. He leaves.

EXT. DEWEY TRAILER HOME—DAY

He goes out and gets in his car.

EXT. HORACE'S HOUSE—DAY

He heads for Horace's house, where he finds his wife's car. He parks, gets out, and approaches the house with the pistol in hand. He half-circles the small house and is about to break a pane to enter when he changes his direction. After some painful thinking, he tosses the pistol off into a small pond, gets back in his car and drives away.

As he drives away he says "Thank you, Jesus" and sings "Precious Memories," an old hymn, to calm himself.

INT. MOTHER'S KITCHEN—DAY

Sonny is having coffee with an old family friend VIR-GIL.

VIRGIL: The best thing is to get out on the road and evangelize, you know, get away.

SONNY: Can't do that, no way. I'd die of loneliness out there. It's bad enough here, but out there, I'd be finished.

Sonny's mother is sitting in the background conveniently eavesdropping.

MRS. DEWEY SR.:   Don't let her have those kids. You fight her for those children, you hear me!

We HEAR a HORN HONK as Sonny jumps up right quick.

MRS. DEWEY SR. *(continuing)*:   Where are you going now, Sonny?

SONNY: Out, Momma! I'm going out!

As he leaves the kitchen, we HOLD ON him as he goes out the front door to get in Joe's car, which is waiting for him. Virgil says:

VIRGIL (V.O.):   Mrs. Dewey, I'll drop by tomorrow. I've got some good sweet corn and summer squash that you could use. I'll be by early, so I'll leave them on the back porch, if you're still asleep.

She thanks him as we . . .

CUT TO:

EXT. DEWEY TRAILER HOME—DAY

As the car pulls up . . .

SONNY *(V.O.)*:   Just sit here in the car and wait, in case I start chokin' this woman to death. If I do, you'll know it!

He walks about eight to ten steps toward the house, turns around and says . . .

SONNY *(V.O. continuing)*:   You hear me?

INT. DEWEY TRAILER HOME—DAY

A rather quiet but tense scene between Sonny and his wife. She watches his hands during the whole scene.

SONNY: For some time.

Jessie nods in the affirmative.

SONNY *(continuing)*:   For a lot longer than this dumb, blind son of a bitch could ever thought about, right?

Jessie looks off.

SONNY *(continuing; looking directly at her)*:   What?

JESSIE: For some time, yes.

SONNY: Well, what are we going to do about all this?

JESSIE: What do you mean?

SONNY: Just what I said.

There is silence for a moment. Jessie shrugs.

SONNY *(continuing)*: What? What's that?

JESSIE: I want out of all this. I just want to be out. That's all.

SONNY: Out of what? This marriage?

JESSIE *(almost inaudible)*: Yes. *(looking down, not very sorrowful, but rather determined)*

SONNY: I'll have to think about that.

JESSIE: Sonny, there's not a whole lot for you to think about. I want to get on with it. And keep your hands right where they are.

SONNY: What? What do you want to get on with?

JESSIE *(very pointed and caustic)*: My life!

SONNY *(to himself)*: That's it.

He looks at her as we CUT TO her holding his gaze.

SONNY *(continuing)*: Now I'm gonna tell you something. *(smiling)* I may make a little noise about all of this, you know that, don't you?

JESSIE: I'm sure you will, Sonny. I'm sure you will.

SONNY: Nobody better mess with my children, especially any puny-assed youth minister, you hear me?

JESSIE: Nobody will, Sonny, I can assure you of that *(a pause)* I wouldn't make over this too much if I were you. I certainly know as much about what you do and have done as you *think* I do, and you know that!

SONNY: Yeah, I guess I do.

JESSIE: Now, as I said, I want to get on with my life.

SONNY: Before I leave this room, would you do me just one favor?

JESSIE: What?

SONNY: Would you get on your knees one more time with me; just this last time. *(he gets on his knees and pulls on her wrist)*

JESSIE: Why, Sonny?

SONNY: Come on!

JESSIE: Why, Sonny?

SONNY: I want the Lord to hear us together in prayer, a prayer of loving understanding, for possible future reconciliation for us and for our son and daughter.

JESSIE: No, Sonny, this isn't the time.

SONNY: Jessie!

JESSIE: No, please, Sonny, I don't want to pray with you today!

SONNY: Tomorrow or maybe next week.

JESSIE: No, Sonny.

SONNY: I see. There hasn't been a problem we haven't been able to solve when we get down to it and you know that.

JESSIE: He's already given me my answers.

SONNY: Our Lord has.

JESSIE: Yes.

SONNY: Are you sure it was the Lord talking?

JESSIE: We've prayed since before we were newlyweds and my knees are worn out over us. I just don't want it this way anymore.

SONNY: Because of my wandering eye and wicked, wicked ways!

JESSIE: Not just that, it goes beyond just that.

SONNY: I love my family, I always have. I have a wandering bug in me, that's why I love to evangelize, but I love my family, I love my wife and my babies. Do you know I love you, Jessie?

Jessie just looks at him.

EXT. MRS. DEWEY SR.'S HOME—DAY

As the car approaches his mother's home:

SONNY (*V.O.*):   What do I need somebody like that for anyways?

JOE *(V.O.)*:   I'm with you all the way, Brother. If it weren't for you showing me the Lord, who knows what jail I'd be in. I'm never going to let you forget that as long as I know you; you hear me now, don't you?

SONNY *(V.O.)*:   I appreciate it. *(beat)* oh-oh!

As the car pulls up to Sonny's mother's home, several more cars can be seen parked on the street in front of the house. Sonny gets out and walks onto the front porch and enters the front door with Joe following.

INT. MRS. DEWEY SR.'S LIVING ROOM—DAY

As he enters the living room, there are five or six CHURCH MEMBERS waiting for him. There is an uncomfortable feeling throughout the scene that is to follow. Faces are long except for Mrs. Dewey Sr., who is in the background, along with Joe, waiting for something to happen now that her son has arrived.

SONNY *(looking at everyone)*:   Whose funeral are we about to attend here—don't tell me it's mine.

CHURCH MAN #1:   Reverend, we have bad news, very bad.

MRS. DEWEY SR.:   You know what that woman has gone and done?

SONNY: Momma, be quiet, we're talking business here.

MRS. DEWEY SR.:   I'm only trying to help.

SONNY: We don't need your help. When we need it, we'll ask for it!

Mrs. Dewey Sr. sits; then trying to cover a slow boil.
The church members look at each other not knowing
how to begin.

SONNY *(continuing)*:   Brother Edwards, what can I do for
you this morning?

EDWARDS: I don't know how to begin this.

SONNY: Open your mouth and just get to it is about the
best way I know.

EDWARDS: It seems that Sister Jessie don't want you
among us anymore, and that she's gonna take the
church away from you through the proper channels.
That's why we're here.

SONNY *(looks at Joe)*:   I just came from there and you all
are here. I was just there and you're here already?

CHURCH WOMAN *(guilt is all around)*:   She wanted it to
come from some portion of the church body, don't
you know?

SONNY: She did? I see. *(keeps nodding his head)*

MRS. DEWEY SR.:   She can't do that, you know that!

SONNY: Oh yes she can. I imagine she can do about anything she wants to at this point. Can't she, Brother
Edwards?

EDWARDS: This all happened too quick-like it seems.

SONNY: You're telling me!

EDWARDS: We didn't know.

SONNY: Didn't know what?

CHURCH MAN #2:   All of the particulars. We still don't know the particulars, at least I don't.

EDWARDS: It seems a proper vote was taken according to the church bylaws. And according to the state laws of Texas for nonprofit organizations. You helped set it up, the way it is.

SONNY: When was this proper vote taken, seeing that I wasn't there?

CHURCH WOMAN: The day before yesterday. That's what we were told.

CHURCH MAN #1 & #2:   We're sorry! This is all such a shock.

EDWARDS: I don't know what else to say at this time. This is a very upsetting thing to have to do . . . to come here like this. *(pause)* There's something so wrong here, so tell us what to do, we'll listen. You have a lot of support from many of our members, you know that don't you? Tell us what you want us to do.

SONNY *(after a moment)*:   I don't know. I don't know. Tell you what—why don't we all just adjourn this gathering—whatever we want to call it—before it turns into another kind of deal. I wouldn't want that and neither would you.

EDWARDS: Well, all right—whatever you think is best.

MRS. DEWEY SR.:   Sonny . . .

SONNY: Mother!!! You've delivered your message and I've received it.

He walks through the kitchen and the back door into the yard.

EXT. BACKYARD—DAY

SONNY *(to himself)*:   She got me by the short hairs. Struck quick, didn't she?

He goes over and fixes a fence post that needs a bit of straightening.

As we HOLD ON HIM with a wide SHOT, his voice begins to come in talking boldly and strongly to God.

DISSOLVE TO:

EXT. FRONT OF HOUSE—NIGHT

We end up in front of the house with one light on in the upper bedroom; we then cut inside to Sonny talking to God.

INT. MRS. DEWEY SR.'S BEDROOM—NIGHT

Mother is sleeping and being awakened by her son's voice coming from the upstairs bedroom.

INT. UPSTAIRS BEDROOM—NIGHT

Sonny is yelling at God for letting him down and letting Satan get the best of him.

SONNY: I can't hardly stand it no more and you let it happen, Lord. Somebody has taken my wife, they've stole my church—a temple I built for you. I'm pretty goddamned mad tonight, Lord. I'm no Communist, no, I'm not. And no, I'm not going to get on my knees, oh no; I'm gonna stand here if it takes all night and yell at you. You let me down. I guess I ain't right some way or other and you let me down. You let the Devil in. Satan has clean jumped in here and caused some kind of havoc. I know you don't fraternize with no satanic forces, God, but what's going on? Satan has messed with me, with my temple, with my family. I'm gonna yell at you 'cause I'm mad at you. I can't take it. Give me some kind of sign or something. Blow this pain out of me—connect me with the Holy Ghost—short-circuit this pain out of me before I expire. Don't play possum on me, you hear me? You're omnipotent, know and see all so I know you're there. Short-circuit this pain with the Holy Ghost. Give it to me, give it to me tonight, Lord God Jehovah. Give me peace, if you won't give me back my wife, give me peace! I don't know who's been fooling with me—you or the Devil. I won't even mention the human involved here, he's just a mutt, so I'm not even going to bring him into it. I'm confused and I'm mad. I'm mad at you. Heal this broken heart. Should I lay hands on myself, what should I do? Deliver me, Lord God, deliver me. I am your servant. Deliver me tonight. Deliver me tonight. We'll try it another way.

I'm not gettin' off my knees until I get a sign. Now, come on—come on—bind up the brokenhearted, I'm your servant, I'm your servant tonight! Let the still small voice of Jesus come into my chest and heart and take away this pain! If you won't give me a sign, then you can take me home tonight. I'll see you face-to-face in the morning, eyeball to eyeball. When I awake in the morning to the archangel and take my first step into the Kingdom. Lord take my breath from me tonight. I'm asking for you to take my life—that I may see my own death tonight. I'm praying for my death—take my life from me so that I can sit and talk with you in the morning.

The mother is smiling—it's good to have him home again. As Sonny awakens and sees that he is not in Heaven, he quietly says, "Momma."

CUT TO:

EXT. FRONT OF TEMPLE—DAY

The car pulls up to the temple.

JOE *(V.O.):* You didn't sleep much?

SONNY *(V.O.):* I haven't slept in forty-eight hours. I was yelling at God 'till sunup.

JOE *(V.O.):* You got the Pentecost croup?

SONNY (V.O.): And how!

Joe and Sonny get out of the car. They are dressed in suits. As they head into the temple:

JOE: Why you going where you're not wanted?

SONNY: Come on, they can't lock me out. They can vote me out, but they can't lock me out! These people love me!

INT. TEMPLE—DAY

Joe and Sonny sit in the back of the temple as the offering is being completed. Sonny suddenly gets up and goes down the aisle. People look at him knowing that there has been a change in the church, as some wonder why he's here and are quite curious as to what he's doing walking down the aisle.

He stops in front of the offering, takes out a fifty-dollar bill, holds it up for all to see, and puts it in the basket. He then goes up on the pulpit, pats the organ player on the back, acknowledges Jessie, and approaches his nemesis. He looks him in the eye, shakes his hand, pulls him in, and hugs him in the spirit of good fellowship. He half-whispers something in his ear, turns around, waves to a few friends, then walks up the aisle and out of the church, with Joe following.

EXT. TEMPLE—DAY

As they get outside, six, seven, or eight PEOPLE come up to him and begin to ask him specific questions. "What's happened?"

SONNY: I'm no longer your local pastor.

SONNY SUPPORTER #1: Why? We didn't vote. How can that be?

SONNY: In a nonprofit organization like this, there are only three votes, Brother. It's a two to one majority. And guess who got the one?

SONNY SUPPORTER #2: You showed 'em with the fifty-dollar bill, Praise God, I sure liked that.

SONNY SUPPORTER #1: What's gonna happen now?

SONNY SUPPORTER #3 (FEMALE): A lot of people will go with you. I know I would if you'd start your own church.

SONNY: This was my own church, Sister, this was my own church.

SONNY SUPPORTER #1: What do you figure you'll do in the immediate future?

SONNY: Well, I'll tell ya, I'm gonna go on home for now and fix my momma some dinner and then I guess I'll just pray on it for a while. God bless you. I love ya.

Sonny and Joe get in their car and drive off as people wave and say good-bye.

INT. LIQUOR STORE—DAY

Sonny picks out a bottle of liquor and pays for it.

CUT TO:

EXT. LIQUOR STORE—DAY

He comes out carrying his bottle. He sees a BLACK MAN preaching. He has two singers with him—one with a tambourine and still another man plays a saxophone. Sonny is delighted to see this, especially since the preacher is preaching very hot and coming off the ground about two feet every time he makes a point. He preaches against the evils of alcohol, against those who use it, and against this store that is selling it! Sonny joins in:

SONNY: Come on, Brother—preach, come on!

When a certain rhythm is punctuated, Sonny responds with a subtle bump and grind as he gets into the spirit. His hands are raised as he participates. He is oblivious to a DERELICT who slips the bottle right out of his hand as he shouts:

SONNY *(continuing)*: Preach, come on, Preacher!

Once there is a lull, Sonny notices that his bottle is missing. He turns in circles, trying to locate it. He finally wanders off a bit puzzled as to the mysterious disappearance of his bottle. He might even turn as an afterthought and go back into the liquor store to buy another bottle. We would see this somewhat in the distance, shooting over the preacher and his small group and into Sonny at the counter in the background.

EXT. CHURCH GROUNDS—DAY

It is 6:45 P.M. as Sonny cruises up to the sight of Dinner on the Grounds. There are a fair number of people still there although it has thinned out somewhat. And in the middle of a gathering of children, Bobby and Little Jess can be SEEN playing. Sonny gets out of his car and proceeds to stroll over to where the children are. He's a slight bit tipsy from his afternoon outing and proceeds accordingly. As he gets closer, Jessie sees him and comes over. She doesn't want him here at all, but does have a certain empathy when she sees him.

JESSIE: I really wish you hadn't come here.

SONNY: I've come to see my babies, Mrs. Dewey, if that's all right with you?

Horace has come over and stands beside Jessie.

HORACE: Is everything all right here?

SONNY: Everything is in order, Rodney.

JESSIE: I'll get them, you all stay here.

She heads off in the direction of Bobby and Jess.

SONNY: Right on, Your Highness, right on!

HORACE: Are you feeling all right?

SONNY: I feel about as good as I've ever felt in my life thus far, Rodney—

He starts for the children.

HORACE: Why don't you stay here, Sonny, and my name's not Rodney.

SONNY *(almost to himself)*:   I want to see my beauties, if you don't mind.

HORACE: I'm really and truly sorry about what's happened. I really am.

SONNY *(this is said so Horace can hear it and nobody else)*:   Why don't you just fuck off before I take my boot here and carve you out a second asshole. *(muttering to himself)* Right where your nose is at.

HORACE: There's really no need for that kind of talk.

Sonny is approaching Jessie and the children. He takes them, and also Jessie, by the arm.

SONNY: Let's all go on home now.

He kind of forces Jessie along with the kids. Horace catches up and tries to intervene. Sonny shoves him and then pushes Jessie on. Horace comes over again. Sonny offhandedly stoops down and comes up with a two-by-four that is laying near a pile of lumber. He swings with a good deal of force and hits Horace right between the eyes.

SONNY *(continuing)*:   One for the road, Rodney.

He grabs Jessie by the hair and drags her toward the car. The children are quite frightened and yell:

CHILDREN: Daddy, don't . . . Don't hurt Mommy! Please Daddy!

Jessie is kicking and screaming.

JESSIE: Let go of me, you son of a bitch. I'll tear your eyes out!

SONNY: Let's go, Momma, time to go home.

JESSIE: Let go of me, you drunken animal!

SONNY: You want to come with me, Rooster?

Boy nods "no."

SONNY *(continuing)*:   OK, honey.

He drags her forward but she beats, claws, and scratches until he lets her go. She runs back to Horace, who is laying on the ground, very unconscious. Sonny drifts off to his car as the children break from him also. There is a good deal of commotion around Horace as people begin to gather. Sonny gets in his car, starts it, and drives off.

As he drives off, we HEAR an ambulance siren coming from the other direction.

CUT TO:

INT. DEWEY TRAILER HOME—DAY

We SEE Sonny come into his house and tear around frantically while he digs up hidden cash from three different places—perhaps a bottle is stashed away with one of the piles. As he is about to leave his home forever, he allows himself to indulge in an almost casual moment as he personally surveys things for the last time.

He walks quickly out the door.

EXT. DEWEY TRAILER HOME—DAY

He heads for his car with whatever cash he may have—$1,700—that will have to last for as long as it lasts.

As Sonny heads toward his car, his NEIGHBOR, although he has his back to Sonny watering his lawn, exchanges pleasantries as Sonny hurriedly gets in the car and drives away.

EXT. FRONT OF JOE'S HOUSE—DAY

Sonny screeches to a stop in front of Joe's house, honks, and gets out, leaving the motor running. He walks halfway to the house as his friend comes out. Sonny motions him back around to the driver's side.

SONNY: Well, I've done it this time.

JOE: What happened?

SONNY *(half smile)*: I let that sucker have it!

JOE: How bad, what happened?

SONNY: I beat him like a stepchild.

JOE: Is he hurt bad?

SONNY: I 'magine. Bad enough.

JOE: Come on, what happened?

SONNY: I think he might be on the road to glory this time.

   Joe looks at him.

SONNY *(continuing)*: I feel it.

JOE: You sure?

SONNY: I feel it. I might of really done it this time. I gotta go.

JOE: Where to?

SONNY: Wherever. This may be it!

JOE: I hope to hear from you, Sonny.

SONNY: I gotta go! Joe, I'm gonna miss my beauties, Praise God! Give 'em my love when you see them.

JOE: You bet.

SONNY: Check on Momma. I can't tell her what I've done. I really can't.

JOE: I sure as hell hope I see you soon.

SONNY: I don't know. I gotta go.

He reaches and pulls Joe through the window for a heartfelt hug.

SONNY *(continuing)*:   God bless you, Brother.

As he drives off . . .

JOE: How can I get in touch with you?

SONNY: I don't know. I gotta go!

CUT TO:

INT. CAR—DAY

Sonny driving. He is very troubled and pensive. He drives and drives. When he comes to a stop sign or red light, he is suspicious of any glance that innocently might come his way. When he passes a police car, he feels like John Dillinger. He knows that his guilt must be like a beacon light, so strong is it to him. He has pulled over to the side of the road and catnapped during the night. This didn't last very long because of his jumpiness at any strange sound that he heard. Mostly he just drives.

INT. CAR—DAY

At one point Sonny turns onto a side road, merely because he sees a police car about to turn onto his road as he reaches an intersection.

INT. CAR—DAY

As he drives down a small county paved road, he

approaches a very small church that is out in the middle of nowhere—Southeast Texas. He stops in the middle of the road and contemplates this Church of God of Prophecy, sitting all alone, with almost sixteen or seventeen cars parked around it. He pulls over, gets out, and goes in.

CUT TO:

INT. CHURCH—DAY

SISTER JEWEL is preaching.

CUT TO:

Sonny watching. It is very basic preaching (with a definite style) and extremely sincere from start to finish.

DISSOLVE TO:

INT. CHURCH LOBBY—DAY

Afterward, Sonny shakes Sister Jewel's hand and thanks her for the service. He tells her that it was the most sincere message he has heard in years.

CUT TO:

EXT. CHURCH PARKING LOT—DAY

Sonny is waiting in his car, as he watches for the last person to leave the small church and drive away. After he is certain everyone has gone, he gets out and heads for the back of the church building.

EXT. CHURCH—NIGHT

He snoops around until he finds a small back door that he jars open. He finds various tools, including an old lawn mower and a pair of clippers.

During a MONTAGE sequence, he cuts the lawn of the church, clips the hedges, and tidies up. He then puts things away, gets in his car, and leaves, never to see the woman or her church again.

EXT. SONNY'S CAR—DAY

Sonny is sitting in his car on the edge of an empty field that lies adjacent to a wooded area. Several night birds can be HEARD, including great horned owls, answering one another. In the distance, we HEAR a quiet and strange HISSING SOUND (probably deer). All of this, in fact, is very settling to Sonny. He sits peacefully, listening. We go back in time.

INT. MRS. DEWEY SR.'S LIVING ROOM—DAY

FLASHBACK

We go back in time to people standing around TWELVE-YEAR-OLD SONNY, who is laid out, motionless upon a table. Possibly, there is a chain of hands being laid on him, perhaps ten or fifteen people at his bedside, all with their hands upon him. But as the DOCTOR enters the room, they all peel off, except for one person, the boy's GRANDFATHER, who for now will be named REV. JACK DEWEY. The doctor has his stethoscope out and is very carefully and scientifically going over the boy. Although the doctor personally is a nonbeliever in faith healing, he is forced to go along with working beside the grandfather, who is sitting at the boy's head, with his hand placed across his forehead. In the background can be HEARD the same small and subtle sounds that are heard in a Pentecostal Church (not so much speaking "in tongues" as just the praising of the Lord and exultations to the Lord Jesus and to the Holy Spirit). It is a quiet noise, but very persistent in that definite, specific drone that is always in evidence in those churches. The doctor leaves the room, the family continues to pray. As the doctor comes back in, we . . .

CUT TO:

INT. MRS. DEWEY SR.'S LIVING ROOM—DAY

As Sonny looks down objectively back upon his own body. Over to one side on the left he can SEE himself with people gathered around him, but on the right he SEES a long, black tunnel with a light at the opposite end. THE CAMERA COMES IN TIGHTER as the doctor bends over the boy, and after examining him again, says, "I don't understand, this boy—his pulse is beginning to become somewhat normal again and before he was—his pulse had decreased. He'd been deceased for seven and a half minutes." The family keeps praying around him.

EXT. FIELD—DAY

Sonny is fixing his car—hood is up.

As the sun rises, there is a rising mist in the fields, and off to the side is another road that leads to a small and narrow marshy bayou that has kingfishers hovering nearby and one lone great blue heron. Also white egrets are SEEN nearby—possibly on the backs of the cattle, depending on how far south the location is.

The SOUNDS of the birds of early morning should emerge out of the calls from the nightbirds.

As we FADE INTO the dawn shot, Sonny is idling his motor for a moment, thinking. He drives to the side road, suddenly picking up a fair amount of speed. He accelerates a bit more as he heads straight for the marshy area. As the car plunges knife-like into the bayou, Sonny rolls out and onto the ground just at the right moment. He gets up and watches the car settle in the early morning mist. He turns and walks straight away as a new man.

He walks a short way and takes out his wallet. He takes out his driver's license, credit cards, any form of identification, and rips them into little bits.

SONNY: You've put up with me for quite a few years, Lord, and I expect you'll be puttin' up with me for a few more . . . *(walking as he talks)*

EXT. FIELD—DAY

MED. WIDE SHOT

of Sonny tossing bits of paper to the early morning breezes. He can be seen saying:

SONNY: Lord, I'm your Apostle now. Whether you want me or not, I'm gonna be your servant, I'm gonna be your Apostle. I'm gonna become worthy of that title. You'll see.

WIDE SHOT

He walks off into the rising sun as the mist now begins to burn off and disappear. He jumps and praises God as he walks away carrying a small bag.

DISSOLVE TO:

EXT. FIELD OF VEGETABLES—DAY

The Apostle walking through a field, stopping, and picking a tomato and an ear of corn—his breakfast. As he eats his morning meal, he takes a shortcut through a wooded area; as he crosses a small meadow, he pauses in the middle of the clearing to finish his tomato.

A VOICE says: "Just keep on a-walkin'" It comes from nowhere, it seems, yet it carries am omnipotent ring in its quiet delivery. Without any hesitation or thought, the Apostle walks quickly away from the area, as we . . .

CUT TO:

EXT. DIRT ROAD—DAY

As the Apostle goes down a dirt road, he sees a BAYOU MAN fishing in a bayou. He walks over and engages himself in a conversation with this fisherman.

E. F. (APOSTLE):   Good morning, my friend.

BAYOU MAN: Mornin'.

E. F. (APOSTLE):   What you catchin' here?

BAYOU MAN: Nuthin' yet.

E. F. (APOSTLE):   You get any freshwater mullet out of here?

BAYOU MAN: Sometimes . . . mostly catfish is here.

E. F. (APOSTLE):   You don't mind if I sit here with you?

BAYOU MAN: No, sir.

They sit a moment in silence.

E. F. (APOSTLE):   You see, I'm on my journey because Satan has driven a big wedge between me and my family. Do you have children?

BAYOU MAN: Yes, sir, and I have eight grandchildren besides.

E. F. (APOSTLE):   So I reckon you would know what it means to face the possibility of losing everybody and everything?

BAYOU MAN *(looks at him)*:   That never happened to me, no sir, but I might could imagine it.

E. F. (APOSTLE):   This bayou is a peaceful place and a beautiful place.

BAYOU MAN: Yes, sir, and it goes on and on back into those woods back yonder.

E. F. (APOSTLE):   I imagine a man could spend hours here in solitude and be happy.

BAYOU MAN: Yes, sir, that's my little camp over there . . .

He points to a small shack about twenty or thirty yards from the bayou, framed by trees and bushes.

BAYOU MAN *(continuing)*:   I spend days and days out here. Then when I feel like it, I just go on back to my wife on the farm, two miles over that way . . . *(points)*

E. F. (APOSTLE):   How do you get there?

BAYOU MAN: I walk.

E. F. (APOSTLE) *(after a long pause)*:   Would you mind if I stayed around here for a day or two, just to rest awhile and get myself ready for whatever the Lord has for me next?

BAYOU MAN: You got no place to go?

E. F. (APOSTLE):   Not that I know of yet, but the Lord is leading me and talking to me.

BAYOU MAN: You sound like a preacher.

E. F. (APOSTLE):   I've been a minister of the Lord since I was twelve years old.

BAYOU MAN: I thought you were.

E. F. (APOSTLE):   I've preached most of my life, but a man has to make ends meet, so's I have about eight trades altogether, for practical purposes.

BAYOU MAN: I know what you mean. *(pause)* I wouldn't know where you'd stay over there. There's only room for me and that's about all.

E. F. (APOSTLE):   I could sleep under one of those bushes over there, make me a bed.

BAYOU MAN *(sizes him up)*:   I got an old pup tent in the back there that my grandchildren play in sometimes.

E. F. (APOSTLE):   You see, I feel like I need to fast for a day or two until I'm ready to go on.

BAYOU MAN: Where to?

E. F. (APOSTLE):   I don't know, but I feel the need to cleanse myself before the next step. One step at a time.

BAYOU MAN: Yes, sir.

DISSOLVE TO:

EXT. BAYOU—NIGHT

Same—later.

E. F. is driving the stakes in the pup tent. There is smoke coming out of the cabin chimney as the old Bayou Man cooks a fish dinner for two.

INT. CABIN—NIGHT

The two men—later.

*Eating—mostly in silence. E. F. makes sounds . . .
"Hmmmmm," "Good," etc.*

INT. TENT—NIGHT—LATER

E. F. settling down in his bed inside the pup tent.

INT. CABIN—NIGHT

*Old Bayou Man looking and listening, and then, as a
precaution, he gets his shotgun and puts it under his
bed.*

EXT. CABIN—DAY

*The Bayou Man is getting his gear ready for another
outing in the bayou. He has finished his breakfast and
is being quiet as he moves around. A VOICE from
inside the tent says:*

E. F. *(offscreen):*   Good morning.

BAYOU MAN: Good morning. I left some breakfast for
you, if you want it.

*(This scene should be between the old Bayou Man
and a tent with a voice.)*

E. F. (*O.S.*): No, I don't believe I will. I started my fast after supper last night.

Bayou Man: I'm coming back about noontime to eat. You don't want no dinner then?

E. F. (*O.S.*): No, sir.

The old fellow walks off to the bayou. We HOLD on the tent for a while and then, for the first time in the scene, we MOVE INSIDE with the CAMERA . . .

INT. TENT—DAY

E. F. is lying on his back with a picture of his wife and children placed in such a way that they are always in his line of vision—if he so chooses to cock his head just a slight bit to the right. E. F. is aware of the lingering breakfast smells that now but faintly permeate the early morning atmosphere. As he looks at his loved ones we . . .

CUT TO:

EXT. TENT—NIGHT

Silent.

INT. CABIN—NIGHT

Old Bayou Man sleeping.

INT. TENT—NIGHT

E. F. sleeping.

CUT TO:

EXT. TENT—DAY

An animal sniffs around the tent. We HEAR a "psst-psst" sound from within the tent, as the animal scurries off into the woods.

INT. TENT—DAY

The Apostle is lying there looking at his loved ones. He sees now only his children, as we SEE that Jessie's face no longer appears alongside of her two children. There are jagged edges where she has been ripped out.

CUT TO:

EXT. TENT—DAY

The old Bayou Man is near the tent.

BAYOU MAN: Mister . . . *(no answer)* Mister . . .

Finally:

E. F. (APOSTLE):   Yes, sir.

BAYOU MAN: Don't you want some of this mullet I caught?

E. F. (APOSTLE) *(pauses)*:   You say you caught some mullet?

BAYOU MAN: Yes, sir.

E. F. (APOSTLE):   I don't believe so, thank you, not right now.

BAYOU MAN: It's here if you want it.

E. F. (APOSTLE):   I can smell it, thank you. *(to himself)* Smells good.

EXT. TENT—NIGHT

We come up at night on the Apostle. He comes out of the tent. In the stillness of the night, he urinates. As he is doing this, the smell of fried oil is still in evidence. He sniffs and sniffs again, and snoops around a bit, then he goes back inside the pup tent.

INT. TENT—NIGHT

E. F. staring ahead, his mind working. We SEE what he sees.

SERIES OF SHOTS:

INT. DEWEY TRAILER HOME—DAY

Close-up on Jessie.

EXT. COUNTRY CHURCH—DAY

FIVE-YEAR-OLD SONNY with BLACK NANNY going into a country church to witness black preacher.

INT. MRS. DEWEY SR.'S BEDROOM—DAY

Sonny's mother on back pointing to heaven.

EXT. TENT—NIGHT

*With a rustling breeze as we HEAR laughter that con-
tinues into the next scene.*

DISSOLVE TO:

EXT. WOODS—DAY

*CAMERA REVEALS the Bayou Man as he tiptoes off
again the next morning. As he walks further and further away we HEAR from the tent:*

E. F. (*O.S.*):   My wife, my wife, my wife, God is my life,
God is my life, my wife, where is my, where is my
wife. *(he sings loudly to comfort himself)* Oh how I
love Jesus.

CUT TO:

INT. WOODS—DAY

*As the Bayou Man comes home with the daily catch,
he stops and watches as E. F. performs a self-baptism.
As he comes out of the water, E. F. keeps walking
and circling and praising God.*

E. F. (APOSTLE):   I believe the Lord wants me to fast until
tomorrow morning and then I think I'll be on my
way.

BAYOU MAN: Where to?

E. F. (APOSTLE):   I don't know yet. But the Lord is gonna
lead me. He led me to you, Brother, and I appreciate
it.

BAYOU MAN: My cousin is a retired pastor. He used to fast once a year to get his mind right.

E. F. (APOSTLE):   Where does he reside?

BAYOU MAN: Pecan Island, Louisiana.

E. F. (APOSTLE):   I never heard of that.

BAYOU MAN: It's a few hours south of here right on the Gulf. He's been there for years now.

E. F. (APOSTLE):   What's his name, maybe I heard of him?

BAYOU MAN: I doubt it, he only had little old churches. Charles Blackwell, he's a first cousin on my mother's side, he used to fast once a year.

E. F. (APOSTLE):   Well, I'm going back in, I guess.

BAYOU MAN: You sure you don't want to end this fast.

E. F. (APOSTLE):   I do, but I won't.

BAYOU MAN *(laughs)*:   Well, it's here if you want it. Is it pretty hot for you in there?

The Bayou Man looks at him.

EXT. TENT—DAY

CAMERA REVEALS a most beautiful bayou sunrise with a faint haze or mist. E. F. comes out of his tent ready to roll. He looks around, and as he is about to leave, he notices a pan of cold perch and corn bread sitting there for him. He gratefully takes it and eats it, chewing carefully and thoroughly. He then turns and walks out of the woods, heading for the county road beyond.

DISSOLVE TO:

EXT. PAYPHONE/EXT. SALOON—DAY

We find the Apostle talking with his mother.

E. F. (APOSTLE): Momma, pray for me, I've done wrong. I may well be a killer, but I am my mother's son, so pray for me, Momma. I want you to know that I love my mother and I love the Lord. *(pause)* Yeah, okay. *(pause)* Me. too. *(pause)* Bye-bye, Momma.

He hangs up, walks into a saloon, and pulls a DRUNK out of the bar. He leaves the drunk standing in the middle of the street, and as E. F. runs to catch his bus, he yells to the drunk "to have strength in the Holy Ghost," and that he "never has to go back in there again."

INT. GREYHOUND BUS—TRAVELING—DAY

A SHORT MONTAGE

Of the bus rolling through various types of country-sides, with different DISSOLVES. OVER the montage should be HEARD a specific GOSPEL SONG, perhaps a beautiful, plaintive one sung by E. F.'s choir.

INT. BUS—TRAVELING—NIGHT

Moving along. Song is now whispered. The CAMERA

REVEALS a MAN looking intently to the back of the bus from his aisle seat three-quarters of the way toward the back. The man just stares for seven or eight seconds of screen time and then gets up to approach what he's staring at. He approaches a sleeping figure stretched out over the whole backseat of the bus. The figure is motionless.

REVERSE ANGLE—the man's face

as he looks down at the sleeping figure. As the man in the standing position is about to lean over and touch the stretched-out figure, the sleeping person rolls over and says:

E. F. (O.S.): Back up about three steps, buddy, or I'll drive your gonads right up into your throat.

It is E. F. heard speaking. The man goes back to his seat and sits down as the bus speeds on into the night.

DISSOLVE TO:

EXT. DRAWBRIDGE—DAY

As the Greyhound bus is about to enter a quiet southwestern Louisiana town, a drawbridge opens and stops it. E. F. gets out and stands on the edge of the wide bayou and watches a totally foreign and novel experience. He watches intently as a Catholic priest blesses the local shrimp fleet. As the drawbridge closes, he gets back in the bus and then proceeds on into town.

EXT. SMALL TOWN—DAY

As the bus stops on the outskirts of a small bayou town in Southwestern Louisiana or Southeastern Texas, the Apostle gets out with his small makeshift bag.

The bus pulls out and leaves him looking around and wondering where to go and what's next. He knows the Lord will lead him. There is a small used car lot adjoining a garage with several gas pumps. Outside of the garage a small man, SAM, is working under the hood of a car. E. F. approaches and asks him if there is a hotel or boardinghouse anywhere in the vicinity.

SAM: When you get into town, there's a motel.

E. F. (APOSTLE): What's the name of it, you remember?

SAM *(pauses)*: I really don't know. I think it's the Red Apple Rest.

E. F. (APOSTLE): What's your problem there?

SAM: Around these points here.

E. F. (APOSTLE): What about them?

SAM: They've just been timed, but there must be something else wrong around there.

E. F. (APOSTLE): Lemme see. You might have an electric problem somewheres.

Sam looks at him.

E. F. (APOSTLE) *(continuing)*: You lost your connection here. Gimme your smallest screwdriver.

He takes the screwdriver and makes the necessary adjustment.

E. F. (APOSTLE) *(continuing)*: See.

SAM: Yeah.

E. F. (APOSTLE): That should do it for now.

SAM: Thank you. I knew it was in there somewhere. I appreciate it.

E. F. (APOSTLE): You betcha, my pleasure.

A head has popped out from a second-story window from a building that joins the garage in the back. This is ELMO, and as he surveys the situation, he asks:

ELMO: How's it coming along? You got it figured out, Sam?

E. F. (APOSTLE): You had an electrical malfunction in the carburetor, but we got her fixed as good as new.

ELMO: Well, great, it looks like we found ourselves a new mechanic. What do you say?

E. F. (APOSTLE): Well, I'm ready if you are.

ELMO: You serious?

E. F. (APOSTLE): Only if you are. You give me the proper parts and I'll build you any vehicle you want from the ground up. *(to Sam)* I'll fix any car you've got.

ELMO: It's up to my partner in the front office. No harm in asking. I doubt it, but it's best to ask anyway. Where you from?

E. F. (APOSTLE): You see where I'm standing, that's where I'm from.

ELMO: Really?

E. F. (APOSTLE): You name it and I been there. I gotta little bit of everywhere in me!

ELMO: Sounds like my first two wives. You get around.

E. F. (APOSTLE) *(joking back)*: I've been in every state except Alaska and a number of foreign countries as well, including Mississippi.

ELMO *(laughs)*: I like it, I like it. Talk to my partner, he knows more about the car end of the business than I do.

HOLD on. His head pops back inside.

CUT TO:

INT. DOWNSTAIRS OFFICE—DAY

E. F. is talking with JACK GUIDRY, Elmo's partner. Guidry is a Texas Cajun and is tall, lean, and rather quiet, especially compared to Elmo.

GUIDRY: We hardly have the work for Sam here. If there's a change or if I hear of anything, I'll get in touch with you. Or you could keep in touch with Sam if you want. I'll tell you though, there's not too much work of any kind around here.

E. F. (APOSTLE):   I appreciate it.

GUIDRY: You bet.

CUT TO:

EXT. SAM'S NEIGHBORHOOD/HOUSE—DAY

Sam and the Apostle are walking down a side street at the end of Sam's working day.

SAM: Where'd you learn about cars?

E. F. (APOSTLE):   My older brother use to race 'em out at Fresno, California. Anything I know, he taught me.

CAMERA REVEALS them coming into Sam's front yard.

SAM: That's it there. I've been working on it since my other car was wrecked.

The yard has a lot of things cluttered around, including parts of old automobiles piled here and there.

By the side of the house is a garage where Sam keeps his car. It's a pretty snazzy-looking thing that he has constructed with a motor from another model that he has been installing.

E. F. (APOSTLE):   By the way, I'm E. F.

SAM: Hi, I'm Sam.

E. F. puts his bag down and they get right to work. The two men work side by side as if they had known each other for some time.

E. F. (APOSTLE):   Now, you're sure it's okay if I stay here, right?

SAM: Don't worry about it, I got plenty of room.

From the time E. F. and Sam introduce themselves a VOICEOVER of E. F. is heard throughout the remainder of the scene.

E. F. (*V.O.*):   Lord, I'm not mad and I'll never be mad at you ever again. I know you're leading me. You led me right to this man, Sam. He's a nice little fellow and a good little fellow and I know you love him tonight just as I know you love me. So whither to ever Thou leadest, I will follow.

CUT TO:

EXT. NEGRO SECTION OF TOWN—DAY

CAMERA REVEALS the Apostle walking through the Negro section of town looking for an address. He goes by a store where several men are sitting around. He asks them a question and they point on down the road. He thanks them and continues on. He asks another person and that person points to a small house that seems to be somewhat neater than some of the others.

E. F. looks at the house for a second and approaches the front porch.

FADE TO:

INT. HOUSE—DAY

The Apostle is seated in a living room with a black man of about sixty to sixty-five, BLACKWELL.

E. F. (APOSTLE):   I had this dream that I would be meeting a man such as yourself. The Lord told me to come right to you . . . *(points directly at him)* When he talks to me I always listen and follow him.

BLACKWELL: Yes, sir, I see.

E. F. (APOSTLE):   In my dream it appeared that I would talk to you about a church or starting a church jointly. Talking at least never hurt nobody, so's I thought we might examine the subject somewhat, reflect on it, you know.

BLACKWELL: Apostle, I don't minister no more. I'm in touch with some of my people, but most are off and joined with other churches.

E. F. (APOSTLE):   If I was to get with some of those people and they was willing maybe to start up a new temple, you know small, would you be willing to come along with me and help me in the community?

BLACKWELL: It's a possibility. You see, I don't preach no more. I had two heart attacks in six months. When I got on the pulpit, I wouldn't hold back and I can't do that no more.

E. F. (APOSTLE):   Amen.

BLACKWELL: I have to take everything a little calmer these days.

E. F. (APOSTLE):   Praise God.

BLACKWELL: I'll pray on it, I will.

E. F. (APOSTLE):   Come on! You might consider it. I mean, I've set up temples all over, you know, all over.

BLACKWELL: That's what I mean. I still don't know why you came to this little old out-of-the-way town here.

E. F. (APOSTLE):   The Lord is leading me, Brother Blackwell, and if I say Satan took my wife and babies, that's all I can say. It's a closed deal and you'll just have to trust me on that. I'm on my own now, but I know I'm with Jesus and when he's by my side I can beat the Devil, loneliness, being alone, whatever. I have him right by my side!

BLACKWELL: Yes, sir, I follow you. Amen. *(pause)* Why should I trust you? Lord knows what you could have done, or been, in the past. Now, you say that God led you to me and not to anybody else?

E. F. (APOSTLE):   Yes, I believe that.

BLACKWELL: If in fact he led you to me, I could accept that. If he didn't, I'll find out soon enough, because he's the one who's gonna let me know one way or the other. And if he did, then naturally I'd want to be with you, wouldn't I? Because then I'd be with him, right? So, in other words, if he's leading you, then he's got to lead me too.

E. F. (APOSTLE):   You put it a lot better than I do, that's for sure.

BLACKWELL: Also, we gotta keep our eye out for the Devil, because if he robbed you of your babies, he could rob someone around here of their babies, especially if he followed you on down here from wherever you're from. *(pause)* Tell you what, I'm gonna keep my eye on you, and the Lord will keep his eye on both of us. And we'll all three look out for the Devil. All right? *(laughs)*

E. F. (APOSTLE):   We got to be careful. I follow you right on. Yes, sir. One other thing, if you know where I might get me a part-time job to help hold me over, I'd appreciate it. Any kind of work. It don't make no difference.

BLACKWELL: I might know, let me see.

CUT TO:

EXT./INT. GARAGE AND RADIO STATION—DAY

The Apostle approaching the garage and radio station. He goes into the front office, nobody is there. He goes through a hallway and finds a SECRETARY working in a rather small back room.

E. F. (APOSTLE):   Good afternoon, I'm E. F. Is Elmo in?

SECRETARY: Hi you—I'm Toosie. He's up there. I'll buzz him for you. He may be on the air at the moment. You can sit down if you like.

E. F. (APOSTLE): Oh, that's all right. You working hard?

TOOSIE: Hardly working. *(laughs)* They keep me pretty busy.

E. F. (APOSTLE): They slave drivers, are they?

TOOSIE: Oh no, we get a lot of things to do, but there's lots of lulls too, you know.

ELMO *(yells down)*: What you got, Toosie?

TOOSIE: E. F.'s here to see you.

ELMO: The Apostle. Send him up.

TOOSIE: Just go on up.

E. F. (APOSTLE): I'll see you in a bit.

TOOSIE: Good to meet you.

E. F. (APOSTLE): Ditto.

INT. ELMO'S OFFICE—DAY

E. F. goes up a steep set of stairs into Elmo's realm. The area is very complete in a modest way, with the proper equipment for broadcasting, etc. The technical side is in order, but the odds and ends that go into making up an office are all around and the place seems a bit messy and cluttered. Elmo greets E. F. in an outgoing and good-natured way.

ELMO: Apostle, good to see you. Good morning.

E. F. (APOSTLE):   Good morning.

ELMO: You feeling all right? What can I do for the Apostle this morning? Sit down.

E. F. (APOSTLE):   How'd you know I was an Apostle?

ELMO: News spreads. What can I do for you?

E. F. (APOSTLE):   I tell you, I would like to find out about buying me some radio time and what kind of setup you have here, etcetera, you know.

ELMO: What did you have in mind?

E. F. (APOSTLE):   Well, I've preached a lot on radio in the past and also a little on cable TV here and there.

ELMO: Good, yeah. *(reaches over and fixes some disks)* Yeah?

E. F. (APOSTLE):   I'd like to see about getting on the radio here for some promotion of a church I'm trying to get going for the Lord. Pentecostal of Holiness is my background. Now, have you had any religious spots in the past that you sold preachers to air on?

ELMO: You bet I have.

E. F. (APOSTLE):   And how did it work out for the most part?

ELMO: Well, I've had a number of preachers in the past. Some good and some not so good.

E. F. (APOSTLE):   How so?

ELMO: As I say, some have worked out fine but others, for instance, have skipped town before they paid me.

E. F. (APOSTLE):   Really?

ELMO: Yeah, so I've learned the hard way that it's got to be a pay-before-you-pray deal. That's what I tell everyone—and there've not been that many lately. *(emphatic)* You pay before you pray. And that's for those who are just looking to pass on through.

E. F. (APOSTLE):   I don't blame you.

ELMO: I've learned to get tough with people or they'll take advantage most every time.

E. F. (APOSTLE):   Right. I'm going to tell you, I'm not just passing through. I'm here to stay.

ELMO *(right at him)*:   Why here?

E. F. (APOSTLE):   I just came and that's it. I can't explain any other way other than the Lord is leading me.

ELMO: I understand. You're out with Sam for the time being.

E. F. (APOSTLE):   That's right. Until I can get situated better.

ELMO: I might be interested, Apostle. We'd have to find some angle of bringing some money in while we're getting the word out over the air, don't you think?

E. F. (APOSTLE) *(overlap)*:   Absolutely. Make ends meet.

ELMO: What kind of preacher are you?

E. F. (APOSTLE):   I can preach on The Holy Trinity, Old and New Testaments, Hell, Resurrection, you name it, I'll give it to you.

ELMO: I see.

E. F. (APOSTLE):   I can preach on the Devil backwards and forwards. I can give you about anything you want to hear.

ELMO *(laughs)*:   Sounds good, sounds good. Now—

He pauses; he is about to bring up the money part.

E. F. (APOSTLE):   I was thinking along these lines. The Lord is leading me, Praise God, I was thinking about making you a deal.

ELMO: I was already coming to that.

E. F. (APOSTLE):   I know you were. *(laughs)* Two guys feeling each other out.

ELMO: What did you have in mind? Let's hear it.

E. F. (APOSTLE):   I was thinking of a trade-off.

ELMO: How so? Preaching for what?

E. F. (APOSTLE):   No, wait. Preaching and working on any of your automobiles that Sam gets stuck on—can't fix, against radio spots for advertising purposes . . . *(pause)* purposes to help build a little temple for our Lord Jesus Christ and keep it alive once it gets going.

ELMO: I like the way you reason and I'm gonna tell you something right off. That's actually not a bad idea at all. Let me get back to you. I'm sure it might work.

I'll run it by my partner. Let me do these spots here. I'll see you later at Sam's.

E. F. (APOSTLE):   All right.

ELMO: I'm pretty sure we can work it out, Apostle. Okay. Oh, by the way, could I call you E. F. for short and not be so formal?

E. F. (APOSTLE):   Surely, but maybe not in public, if you don't mind.

ELMO: Oh, no, no that's what I was gonna say—never in public, oh no, no way, Apostle. Just among friends, if that's all right with you?

E. F. comes down to the . . .

INT. OFFICE—DAY

TOOSIE: How long will you be around for?

E. F. (APOSTLE):   Oh, for quite a while, I'd say.

TOOSIE: Really?

E. F. (APOSTLE):   Yeah.

TOOSIE: I hear you're trying to get a church started around here.

E. F. (APOSTLE):   Yeah, I am. How'd you know that?

TOOSIE: I heard.

E. F. (APOSTLE):   News travels fast! Actually, that's why I'm here, to see if I can get on the radio and do a little spreadin' of the word. Do a little good.

TOOSIE: You getting right after it. Do you always do things that way?

E. F. (APOSTLE): How's that?

TOOSIE: Do you always plunge right in like that?

E. F. (APOSTLE): Well, I tell you, I always get the feeling that if I don't move quick, it might be all over.

TOOSIE: In what way?

E. F. (APOSTLE): Just what I said, 'cause you never know how long the Lord's gonna let you hang around, if you know what I mean.

TOOSIE: Yeah, I do. I think I do.

A moment between them. PHONE RINGS.

TOOSIE *(continuing)*: I'd better take this call.

E. F. (APOSTLE): You never know. *(mouths)* I'll see you later.

He exits.

CUT TO:

EXT. CANE FIELD—DAY

E. F. is revealed cutting sugarcane on a tractor, working alongside black LABORERS. E. F. works with a peaceful smile on his face.

EXT. FRONT OF CHURCH—DAY

Blackwell and E. F. pull up to an old church that's been boarded up.

EXT. CHURCH—DAY

BLACKWELL: I pastored here for over twenty-seven years 'til my health broke down.

E. F. (APOSTLE):   Where is everybody gone to—your flock?

BLACKWELL: They all spread out or gone on. I don't know if you'd want it or be interested in it. It's just a thought.

E. F. (APOSTLE):   All right, all right, yes, sir, glory!

E. F. walks and backs around the little church briskly, looking at it intently.

E. F. (APOSTLE) *(continuing)*:   Here's what I need. Resurrection time, resurrection time. I'll need twenty-nine gallons of white paint, about six gallons of yellow paint for the trim. *(jumps up and down)* I'll need a fair amount of roofing material obviously. It'll come out of my first two paychecks, third if necessary.

BLACKWELL: There's no rent because it belongs to me.

E. F. (APOSTLE):   Bless you.

BLACKWELL: But there are a few back taxes due, that's all!

E. F. (APOSTLE):   I'll take care of that. If I have to, I'll get another job. I can set these churches up in my sleep, no problem. No problem!

BLACKWELL: You move faster than any man I've ever seen.

E. F. (APOSTLE):   Well, I tell everybody, when I was young, I quit school because I didn't like recess.

They laugh.

CUT TO:

EXT. TOWN—NIGHT

Blackwell drops E. F. off near a phone booth in town and waves good-bye. E. F. walks past a crawfish feast and goes to make his phone call.

CUT TO:

EXT. PHONE BOOTH—NIGHT

E. F. on the phone:

E. F. (APOSTLE):   You hold it against me, don't you?

JOE *(V.O.):*   No way, I might of done the same thing, Sonny. I just want you to be all right 'cause I love you.

E. F. (APOSTLE):   You say he's still in a coma?

JOE *(V.O.):*   Yeah, but they say he's showing marked improvement.

E. F. (APOSTLE):   I'm glad to hear that.

INTERCUT:

INT. JOE'S ROOM—NIGHT

JOE: This whole church is praying for him round the clock in one-hour prayer shifts.

E. F. (APOSTLE): Any sympathy I might have had I'm sure is gone by now.

JOE: Yeah, well, pretty much.

E. F. (APOSTLE): I'm gonna pray for him, too.

JOE: That's really nice of you, Brother Dewey. God bless you.

E. F. (APOSTLE): You say the police have questioned you? Maybe I shouldn't call you anymore.

JOE: Maybe for a while. They came by and asked me some questions. I told 'em I didn't know where you are, which is the truth, actually.

E. F. (APOSTLE): Maybe everything is gonna turn out all right.

JOE: I don't know about that. Wherever you are, stay there because they are looking for you.

E. F. (APOSTLE): How you feeling?

JOE: I'm doing fine.

E. F. (APOSTLE): Let me ask you something? How come I haven't been able to get ahold of Momma? I've tried quite a few times and there's no answer.

JOE: I've been meaning to tell you.

E. F. (APOSTLE):   What?

JOE: Your mother's not doing too well; she's in the hospital and I didn't know how to get ahold of you.

E. F. (APOSTLE):   What's wrong?

JOE: I don't know what it is; it's something to do with her kidneys, I think.

E. F. (APOSTLE):   I'll call her.

JOE: You better not, they're all over the switchboards.

E. F. (APOSTLE):   Go visit her for me.

JOE: I already have.

E. F. (APOSTLE):   I love you, Joe, but I got to go.

JOE: You take care, Sonny, and be careful.

He hangs up. We . . .

CUT TO:

EXT. BLACKWELL'S BACKYARD—DAY

Sam, E. F., and Brother Blackwell are painting an old stump of a bus that is sitting and aging in the black preacher's backyard. Little BLACK CHILDREN peer through the fence (and may even come on over) as the optimistic trio paints and works away. The banter is light and full of good fellowship. Sam and Brother Blackwell are painting such things as "Jesus the same, yesterday, today, and forever," "Apostle E. F.," and the address of the temple. The Apostle is working away under the hood of the bus that is being reborn.

E. F. (APOSTLE): Maybe someday we could start an orphanage?

BLACKWELL: One thing at a time, Apostle.

E. F. (APOSTLE): I know, I know. Maybe a year from now. It's just that I'd like to do something for the homeless and fatherless. When Satan robs you of your children it makes you want to truly help others.

BLACKWELL: It all takes money. We'll get there. It all takes time.

E. F. (APOSTLE): We can create interest on local radio here. Elmo's gonna plug us and also in the newspaper. We have a newspaper, don't we? The Lord's moving in me, telling me things. Movin' in all of us. Lean on that brush, Sam.

BLACKWELL: There you go. Praise God!

E. F. (APOSTLE): We'll have dinner on the grounds, we could have softball going on, I pitch a good curveball, we could play the Methodists, sell tickets, get some publicity.

BLACKWELL: Don't get ahead of yourself.

E. F. (APOSTLE): They'll know we're here. We'll show the community that the Holy Rollers is here to stay. Can't get rid of us! He's gonna keep on telling us and speaking to us.

He does a little dance in the spirit with a "Praise God."

BLACKWELL: That reminds me of a story on the Holiness people.

He tells a humorous tale as they all laugh.

MOTHER BLACKWELL comes out with an inviting pitcher of homemade lemonade for the three workers. As they take their lemonade break the small children come closer and . . .

CUT TO:

INT. RADIO STATION—DAY

As we PULL BACK the CAMERA REVEALS the Apostle preaching over the air. He is going at it hot and heavy, and since he has been at it for a good ten minutes, he is perspiring lightly.

Brother Blackwell is seated and seems pleased by what he sees and is hearing. Toosie has just delivered some things to Elmo and is on her way back downstairs but she can't go. She just stops and watches the Apostle go on and on about Elijah in the Old Testament. As he finishes his sermon, he announces that their first service will be held within a month, that the Lord hasn't as yet revealed the time or the place but we're praying on it and your prayer of support would certainly be appreciated. As soon as it is revealed we'll be letting all of the radio audience know immediately. He then hands the microphone to Elmo who reemphasizes the previous announcement. He then reminds them of donations or tithes that would be greatly appreci-

ated at this time. Elmo stays on the air while E. F. goes out and shakes hands with Brother Blackwell. The Brother congratulates him on a job well done. Elmo says a word or two to him while a song is being played on the air.

ELMO: Good job, E. F., we'll see if we can't get those tithes rolling in. I'll see you later.

E. F. (APOSTLE): You betcha. It went great!

Blackwell and E. F. go downstairs.

INT. GARAGE/RADIO STATION—DAY

He surprises Toosie by grabbing her from behind and saying:

E. F. (APOSTLE): How'd I do?

TOOSIE: It seemed you did fine to me.

E. F. (APOSTLE): You reckon?

TOOSIE: I've never heard anyone speak that way before. The preachers I've heard have always just more or less talked, you know. I was actually fascinated by it.

E. F. (APOSTLE): Well, you come to our church when it's ready and I guarantee you won't see nobody sittin' on their hands, will you, Brother Blackwell?

BLACKWELL *(chuckles)*: Not too many.

E. F. (APOSTLE): I don't believe in going to no church in a morgue.

TOOSIE: I can believe that.

E. F. (APOSTLE): Anyways, I'm gonna get you out for dinner sometime before church. That way you won't get scared off. What do you say? I promise you I'll be quiet at you across the table.

TOOSIE: That might be nice, we'll see.

E. F. (APOSTLE): Well, we'll see you all later, you hear?

TOOSIE: Bye-bye.

CUT TO:

EXT. CHURCH—DAY

We find Brother Blackwell watching as Sam is on a homemade scaffold painting while E. F. is on the roof of his church hammering in nails.

INT. CHURCH—DAY

Close on a picture of Jesus—a pair of hands is dusting the face of the picture. We hear the voice of Mother Blackwell: "Lord, you're looking good today, we're proud to have you looking down on us. We love you!" We PULL BACK as she hangs the framed picture behind the pulpit area. As the CAMERA WIDENS, we see between a dozen to fifteen NEIGHBORHOOD CHILDREN working away, getting the church in order. Some are scrubbing on hands and knees, some dusting, some sweeping, some upon boxes cleaning windows. As they all work they chant the books of the Bible from beginning to end in the form of a RAP SONG.

DISSOLVE TO:

EXT. CHURCH—DAY

E. F. and Sam are still working away. We hear the children from the inside and as they reach the end of the New Testament (E. F. begins to recite with them), they burst out of the front doors and look up at the Apostle as they keep repeating "Revelation, Revelation," etc. E. F. takes out a fistful of one-dollar bills and floats them down to the children below. They in turn jump up and grab the falling money, repeating, "Revelation, Revelation!"

DISSOLVE TO:

INT. METAL FOUNDRY—DAY

CAMERA REVEALS the Apostle working in a metal foundry. As he works a MAN comes up to him and whispers something in his ear. E. F. immediately stops what he's doing and follows the man OUTSIDE.

EXT. METAL FOUNDRY—DAY

We see the Apostle from a distance administering to a LARGE MAN. E. F. goes to the man and squats down by him.

E. F. (APOSTLE): Would you like me to pray for you, Buddy?

LARGE MAN: Anything to stop this blood, if you think you can.

E. F. (APOSTLE):   Well, I can't, but I'll tell you what, the Lord can and will stop it! All we got to do is trust, you and me.

Large Man looks at him.

E. F. (APOSTLE) *(continuing; takes a small Bible from a bag)*: Now I want you to listen and hear this. *(he reads from Ezekiel 16:6)*

As he reads, a large, DARK-HAIRED MAN approaches. He observes the proceedings. E. F. finishes reading.

LARGE MAN: It's almost stopped, just like that.

E. F. (APOSTLE) *(quietly)*: Hallelujah, praise God. Say "Thank you, Jesus."

LARGE MAN: Thank you, Jesus.

E. F. (APOSTLE):   Say it again!

LARGE MAN *(a bit embarrassed)*:   Thank you, Jesus.

E. F. (APOSTLE):   You just stay here for a minute before you move, you gonna be all right!

DARK-HAIRED MAN *(interrupting)*:   I've warned you about healing on the job.

E. F. (APOSTLE):   Yes, sir.

DARK-HAIRED MAN: You have anything to say for yourself?

E. F. (APOSTLE):   No, sir.

DARK-HAIRED MAN: Then pick up your pay, preacher. I don't want to see your face around here no more.

We HOLD on E. F.'s face as we

CUT TO:

INT. RADIO STATION—NIGHT

E. F. on the air with Elmo.

E. F. (APOSTLE): We now have our building for our church site, we're working on it day and night and by next week we'll be announcing the exact time of our first service at "The Temple of the Living God," at 4012 South 4th Street, where we certainly hope to worship a God that is alive now and forever more. Our house of worship welcomes you one and all in the name of our Lord and Saviour Jesus Christ, who is the same yesterday, today, and forever.

CUT TO:

EXT. TEMPLE—DAY

A group of PEOPLE are seen hoisting up a sign with an arrow pointing skyward that reads, "One Way Road to Heaven."

INT. RESTAURANT—NIGHT

E. F. and Toosie are in a modest restaurant in the middle of town.

E. F. (APOSTLE): What do you think you're gonna have?

TOOSIE *(friendly banter):* Give me a chance to read the menu.

E. F. (APOSTLE):   Oh, right. I know what I'm gonna have.

He looks at her over the menu, sizing her up.

TOOSIE: What?

E. F. (APOSTLE):   I'm gonna have me some of these gulf shrimp.

TOOSIE *(sensing his gaze)*:   I guess I'll have the same thing.

E. F. (APOSTLE):   You sure?

TOOSIE: Yeah, that'll be fine.

The WAITRESS writes the order down and leaves. Pause. E. F. smiles.

TOOSIE *(continuing; laughing)*:   What?

E. F. (APOSTLE):   Nothing. *(laughing)* Whatever made you move down here?

TOOSIE: My husband had a good offer on the offshore crew boats.

E. F. (APOSTLE):   Your husband? *(ducks to one side; looks around like "where is he?")* I guess that's the end of this deal.

TOOSIE *(laughs)*:   No, we're kind of separated at the moment.

E. F. (APOSTLE):   Kind of separated, you say?

TOOSIE: We're trying to see if it's gonna work out or not.

E. F. (APOSTLE):   Experimenting.

TOOSIE: I don't know if it's going to work or not, we'll see.

E. F. (APOSTLE): Oh, Lord, please let it work in my favor. You have any kids?

TOOSIE: I have two boys that stay with my mother.

E. F. (APOSTLE): Where at?

TOOSIE: In Bowling Green, Kentucky. *(pause)* You ask a lot of questions.

E. F. (APOSTLE): Do I? I guess I do. I've evangelized there a time or two.

TOOSIE: It seems to me there were a lot of preachers coming through there when I was a girl.

E. F. (APOSTLE): I coulda been one of them. It's been a while.

TOOSIE: Do you have any children?

E. F. (APOSTLE): I have a boy and a girl. My beauties, I call them, my beauties.

TOOSIE: Where do they live?

E. F. (APOSTLE): They live a long ways away, same as yours—yeah—Do you miss your babies a lot?

TOOSIE: Yes, I do. They're not exactly babies, but I do miss them.

E. F. (APOSTLE): Ditto.

TOOSIE: What?

E. F. (APOSTLE): I said ditto.

TOOSIE: Oh.

E. F. (APOSTLE):   So, you think I'm a good date. What do you think?

TOOSIE: What do you mean?

E. F. (APOSTLE):   How am I doing so far?

TOOSIE: You're not suppose to ask that.

E. F. (APOSTLE) *(kidding her)*:   I'm not?

TOOSIE: No, you're supposed to let the evening develop and draw your own conclusion.

E. F. (APOSTLE):   You think?

TOOSIE: I wouldn't have gone out with you if I didn't think you were going to be . . . *(pause)*

E. F. (APOSTLE):   You like me, don't you?

TOOSIE *(looks at him)*:   Stop looking at me like that.

E. F. (APOSTLE):   Like what?

TOOSIE*(looks off)*:   Never mind.

> *The waitress brings the two shrimp dinners and serves them to E. F. and Toosie. Toosie is about to pick up her fork and begin. E. F. subtly and easily prevents her from starting to eat. He says a short and appropriate grace.*

E. F. (APOSTLE):   Lord, we thank you for this food we are about to receive into our bodies. We thank you for this spiritual fellowship between a good woman and a good man. I ask that you show us the light in guidance and that you may lead each of us daily so that we may more clearly see the path that you have set down for us throughout all time and eternity. We thank you for this day in Jesus' name, Amen. Now you can eat, woman!

They both begin to eat.

DISSOLVE TO:

EXT. ROAD—NIGHT

We PAN with Sam's car, borrowed for the evening, as E. F. drives Toosie home.

E. F. *(V.O.):* You used to be religious?

TOOSIE *(V.O.):* No, I always was, but I only used to like the hymns and the singing.

E. F. *(V.O.):* Really?

TOOSIE *(V.O.):* Yeah, every night when I was real young, my mother would sing "I Love to Tell the Story."

E. F. *(V.O.):* That's nice, that's always been a favorite in my family, too.

They start to sing it together as we . . .

DISSOLVE TO:

INT. CAR—NIGHT

It pulls up to Toosie's little house.

E. F. (APOSTLE):   Well, what do you think? Is this going to be it?

TOOSIE *(puzzled)*:   What do you mean?

E. F. (APOSTLE):   I guess this is it.

TOOSIE: Why?

E. F. (APOSTLE) *(plays with words)*:   I won't be seeing you anymore.

TOOSIE *(laughs)*:   Of course you'll be seeing me again. I'll be seeing you all the time.

E. F. (APOSTLE):   You can't see me like a date anymore with your husband and all, can you?

TOOSIE: I'll have to think about it. I told you we're separated.

E. F. (APOSTLE):   But you can't see me, this is the end.

TOOSIE: I told you we'd see, silly.

She takes his hand in hers. They look at each other.

TOOSIE *(continuing)*:   I had a real nice time, real nice.

E. F. (APOSTLE):   Did you, really?

TOOSIE: Yes, I did.

E. F. (APOSTLE):   Me, too . . . *(edges closer)* You make me feel good, you know that, really good.

TOOSIE: Do I?

E. F. (APOSTLE):   Yes, ma'am, you do.

They have a warm feeling between them as they both look at their hands that are together.

E. F. (APOSTLE) *(continuing)*: I guess I'll see you in a day or two.

They look into each other's eyes.

E. F. (APOSTLE) *(continuing)*: I hope so.

E. F. puts his arm around her and goes to kiss her. Just as their lips are about to meet, she turns away at the last second. He then goes to her lips again and she snaps her head back the other way. It becomes a gentle dodging match that people often experience on first dates. Finally, he gives up and says:

E. F. (APOSTLE) *(continuing)*: Well, give me a hug at least. Now I can have a hug, can't I?

TOOSIE: Oh-oh-oh, of course you can.

They hug and coo for a moment. Eventually she gets out after she kisses him on the cheek.

TOOSIE *(continuing)*: I had a super time.

E. F. (APOSTLE): Can I see you again?

TOOSIE: We'll see. Bye-bye.

She gets out and goes to her front door and lets herself in. E. F. drives away, exhaling an exasperated sigh.

CUT TO:

INT. CAR—NIGHT

E. F. is driving. He pulls into a deserted filling station. He is very lonely as he stops by a public phone booth.

INT. PHONE BOOTH—NIGHT

He goes into the phone booth and calls Jessie back in Ft. Worth. When he hears her voice on the other end he just stands there silently.

INT. DEWEY TRAILER HOME—NIGHT

INTERCUT Jessie on the other end.

JESSIE: Who is this?

He listens for a while and then hangs up.

Jessie hangs up; reacting.

The Apostle leaves the booth and heads for his car. He suddenly stops, turns around, and goes back into the booth.

INT. PHONE BOOTH—NIGHT

He picks up the phone and dials quickly. He breathes heavily, flexes, and then waits.

E. F. (APOSTLE):   Hey, you, Toosie, how are you?

TOOSIE *(V.O.)*: Where are you?

E. F. (APOSTLE): I'm in a phone booth by the Jack in the Box out on the road here in the cold.

TOOSIE *(V.O.)*: You are?

E. F. (APOSTLE) *(pauses)*: Yeah and I'm coming right on over to your house, right now. I want to see you!

TOOSIE *(V.O.) (pause)*: I'm sorry, E. F. I really can't. I have to get up early.

E. F. (APOSTLE) *(groans)*: Well, you're right. I should never of said that, should I? That wasn't right of me.

TOOSIE *(V.O.)*: No, that's all right.

E. F. (APOSTLE): Then I'm coming on over, no I'm not, no I'm not. I didn't say that. Did I say that?

TOOSIE *(V.O.)*: I'm sorry.

E. F. (APOSTLE): I'm not a bad guy for asking, am I?

TOOSIE *(V.O.)*: Of course not, silly.

E. F. (APOSTLE): I guess I better go on now. You're a good woman. You know that?

TOOSIE *(V.O.)*: And you're a good man.

E. F. (APOSTLE): No, I'm not.

TOOSIE *(V.O.)*: Yes, you are. I'll see you at the office I hope.

E. F. (APOSTLE): Oh, I'll be around, you'll be seeing me.

TOOSIE *(V.O.)*: Good night, E. F.

E. F. (APOSTLE):   Good night, Toosie.

He thinks for a moment after he hangs up and we . . .

CUT TO:

EXT. CHURCH—NIGHT

E. F. drives up to his little church. It is completely dark. He goes into the church and lights the sign that says, "One-way road to Heaven." He comes outside to see the effect. He then praises God as the light flashes on and off.

CUT TO:

INT. BLACKWELL KITCHEN—DAY

E. F. getting ready for his first live sermon as the Apostle. He is sitting in the Blackwell kitchen getting his hair styled by MOTHER BLACKWELL.

BLACKWELL: We've covered almost everything.

E. F. (APOSTLE):   You reckon?

BLACKWELL: We're gonna be fine as long as we trust Him. There's no other way we can look. And if the bus doesn't break down.

E. F. (APOSTLE) *(grunts and chuckles)*: Right on!

As Mother Blackwell finishes, she holds up an old mirror and says:

MOTHER BLACKWELL: What do you think, Apostle?

E. F. (APOSTLE):   That's just fine, Sister Blackwell, just fine and dandy. Thank you.

MOTHER BLACKWELL: You're welcome.

As E. F. gets up, he puts his jacket on and says:

E. F. (APOSTLE):   We better get going.

BLACKWELL: Yes, sir.

They walk through the sitting room and out the front door.

EXT. BLACKWELL HOUSE—DAY

The two ministers march down the sidewalk praising and exalting God—a mighty pair—as they approach the newly renovated bus that is parked in front of Brother Blackwell's house.

CUT TO:

INT. RADIO STATION—DAY

Elmo on the air. He is speaking into his microphone.

ELMO: Even as I speak here today, the Apostle E. F. is making his rounds in his own private bus to bring you physically to his ministry, down on 4012 South 4th Street at his newly renovated Holiness Temple. He is co-pastoring with the Reverend C. Charles Blackwell . . .

EXT. STREET—BUS—DAY

Elmo's V.O. continues as the Apostle guns the motor on his religiously painted bus and takes off down the street with Brother Blackwell. As he turns the corner he knocks over a large garbage can full of trash as he tentatively proceeds down the next block.

ELMO *(V.O.)*: You all are not only safe in his hands, but you are truly in God's hands on this day of worship here in Pecan Island, Louisiana. Remember, for just one month for both the Sunday services, 10:45 A.M. and 7:45 P.M., and the Wednesday evening service at 7:45 P.M., the Apostle E. F. will pick you up personally at the very spot designated for each and every one of you approximately one half hour before the start of each service. And each passenger will receive a small rose of Sharon from the Apostle himself. And those who play, remember to bring your instruments. Praise God! It's a beautiful day, just a few clouds that should disappear by mid-afternoon and with temperatures in the mid-seventies. Have a good day and God bless you one and all!

During Elmo's announcement, the bus has stopped for one or two ladies who have hailed E. F. down. As they get on, the Apostle presents each of them with a small rose of Sharon.

As they pull away from the second stop, a little old black lady, SISTER DELILAH, chases after the bus and yells at the Apostle to wait for her; she waves her hand-

kerchief and shouts until he takes notice of her and stops. She gets on.

INT. BUS—CONTINUOUS—DAY

Sister Delilah chatters away as she sits down behind Brother Blackwell, whom she knows from the past. A fat lady, SISTER JOHNSON, recognizes her.

SISTER JOHNSON: What're you doin' here?

SISTER DELILAH: Same as you, goin' to church.

DISSOLVE TO:

EXT. TEMPLE—DAY

THE LITTLE BUS

As it pulls up in front of the "Temple of the Living God."

There are only seven or eight passengers, all black and one white. As they file out of the bus, the Apostle helps them down the stairs. When they are out, they all head for the church where little Sam takes his turn in ushering them through the front door. Sam is scrubbed and in the only suit he could manage to scrape together.

E. F. gives Brother Blackwell a quizzical look.

BLACKWELL: I know what you're thinking, Apostle, and all I can say is, when you've been on the radio, most all of the white people think that you're black, and most colored people know you ain't black, but they sure do like your style of preaching. So what you see, is what you got!

Both men grin and proceed into the church building.

INT. CHURCH—DAY

The Apostle is reading from the 150th Psalm.

E. F. (APOSTLE):   "Praise ye the Lord, praise God in his sanctuary: Praise him with the sound of the trumpet." Do we have a trumpet?

A little OLD BLACK MAN toots a single note on an old short coronet.

E. F. (APOSTLE) *(continuing)*:   "Praise him with a psaltery and harp." *(he looks around)* No harp. "Praise him with a timbrel"—Do we have a timbrel? *(he points)*

A YOUNG BOY rattles a timbrel.

E. F. (APOSTLE) *(continuing)*:   "Praise him with stringed instruments."

A MAN strums a guitar.

E. F. (APOSTLE) *(continuing; reading from Psalms)*:   "Let every thing that hath health praise the Lord. Praise ye the Lord."

The CAMERA COMES UP on the Apostle talking to his congregation. He is very sincere and warm with them. He goes to them and all join hands.

E. F. (APOSTLE) *(continuing; quotes the scripture):*   Wherever two or more are gathered in my name there will be I also. Remember, my beloved brethren, we are heirs of God and joint heirs with Christ. We are all living and glorifying the one God above, and we will build this church and continue its existence on this very premise.

He calls everybody up to join arms and hug each other's necks. He and they begin to sing "Alleluia."

THE CONGREGATION

Responding. One OLD BLACK MAN has nodded off to sleep as we . . .

CUT TO:

INT. FROSTEE FREEZE—DAY

CAMERA REVEALS the Apostle working in a Frostee Freeze in a white uniform and hat, dishing up ice cream to make milk shakes for the waiting customers.

DISSOLVE TO:

INT. SAM'S HOUSE—NIGHT

E. F. IN BED

Staring at the ceiling.

E. F. (APOSTLE):   Forgive me, Lord, for I know not what I did. Thou shalt not kill. Thou shalt not kill.

CUT TO:

SERIES OF SHOTS: MOS

As E. F. is HEARD on the radio again, we SEE:

EXT. DOCKS—DAY

VIETNAMESE WOMEN cleaning fish, listening.

EXT. CAJUN HORSE RACE—DAY

A Cajun backyard horse race.

EXT. PORCH—OLD AGE HOME—DAY

Front porch of an old age home.

EXT. VIETNAMESE FISHING BOAT—DAY

A Vietnamese fishing boat in the Gulf as the Apostle blares away.

EXT. TRACTOR—DAY

An OLD BLACK MAN driving a tractor with his head-phones on.

CUT TO:

INT. TEMPLE—DAY

A LARGER CONGREGATION

*Where everyone is singing and there is the begin-
nings of a choir in evidence. Everyone is singing in
the spirit.*

CUT TO:

EXT. FLOWING RIVER—DAY

*CAMERA REVEALS the Apostle baptizing a dozen
or more people in a flowing river. The SINGING
from the previous scene continues over this baptism scene. The light should be special for the
scene and the Apostle and some of the people being baptized should be quite chilly from the nippi-
ness in the air.*

DISSOLVE TO:

INT. TEMPLE—NIGHT

*We FIND the Apostle singing along with his choir of
eight or ten people. The Apostle counts the number
of people in the congregation as he sings. They sing
a wonderful old upbeat gospel song. There is a
heavyset man on the guitar and a woman with a
beehive hairdo playing the piano. One elderly gentleman plays the fiddle and an older black man plays
a short coronet. The music is wonderful. As they sing,
one TROUBLEMAKER in the back is standing and
calling out to the pastor:*

TROUBLEMAKER:　What does E. F. stand for? Why don't you give out your full name? Hey, Apostle, it's you I'm talking to. Yes, you, E. F.

The Apostle is fully aware of the man, as are some of the members of the congregation. Every few minutes the man yells out "What does E. F. stand for, are you ashamed to let us all know?"

Eventually E. F. leaves the pulpit and walks down to the front of the church to speak to the man. Sam has followed him.

It might be added here that sometime after the service has started and without anyone noticing her entrance, Toosie has quietly entered the little church and has seated herself off to one side in the back.

E. F. walks the fellow out the front door and asks him what his problem is. Sam is standing nearby listening.

TROUBLEMAKER *(continuing)*:　I don't have a problem. You do.

E. F. (APOSTLE):　No, sir, I don't think I do. I don't think worshiping the Lord is any kind of problem.

TROUBLEMAKER:　Then why don't you let us know what E. F. stands for?

E. F. (APOSTLE):　That's no concern of yours and now I wish you'd either leave these premises or if you decide you want to come back into our church as a gentleman this time, then that's all right too.

TROUBLEMAKER: I'm not going into any man's church with a name like E. F. and I don't particularly want to sit with a bunch of niggers to begin with.

E. F. (APOSTLE): Just get out of here then!

TROUBLEMAKER: I'll go when I so choose, Mr. E. F.

E. F. (APOSTLE): I'd like to talk to you around on the other side.

EXT. TEMPLE—NIGHT

He helps the Troublemaker around to the side of the building. Sam goes to go with him but the Apostle tells him to wait.

The one black USHER that has witnessed the confrontation looks a bit concerned as E. F. and the stranger disappear into the shadows of the little church building.

We INTERCUT the scuffling outside with the small choir on the inside. The choir should disband one by one "in the Spirit" so that by the time the Apostle reappears, there will be no more choir singing as he takes his place behind the pulpit.

USHER AND SAM'S P.O.V.

We HEAR scuffling and thumps and thuds and scraping of feet and a number of grunts accompanied by short gasps of breath. In a few moments or less, the Apostle emerges from the shadows with his suit rum-

pled quite a bit. If one could get a closer look it would be clear that the Apostle is sporting a red eye that is turning blacker by the second.

SAM: What happened?

E. F. (APOSTLE):   Oh, the Lord had me perform an exorcism. It took a little longer than I had hoped.

SAM: An exorcism?

E. F. (APOSTLE):   Yeah, every now and then we have one of them in our churches.

SAM: How did you do it?

E. F. (APOSTLE):   There's no particular ceremony involved. I just put his lights out.

Usher laughs.

SAM: Really?

E. F. (APOSTLE):   Every man has a chin, don't he?

They go back into the church.

INT. TEMPLE—NIGHT

The CAMERA picks him up as he walks back down the aisle to the pulpit area. As he joins in the singing, he sees Toosie for the first time sitting by herself in the back.

The Apostle tells everyone to turn to page such-and-such in their hymnals. They all begin to sing the old favorite that Toosie had told E. F. about in the car on the way home from their dinner date ("I Love to Tell the Story"). He smiles as they sing it, as does she. He tells them all to raise their hands to God as they sing, to sing to his glory.

During the scene the Apostle has dabbed his black eye several times with his handkerchief.

CUT TO:

EXT. TEMPLE—NIGHT

E. F. AND TOOSIE

Walking to a strategic spot where they can look back at the little Temple, which is dimly lighted by a lone street light.

TOOSIE: I enjoyed it.

E. F. (APOSTLE):   Did you?

TOOSIE: Yes. It's been a long time since I've been in church.

E. F. (APOSTLE):   Did you like the music?

TOOSIE: Yeah, it gave me nice warm feelings, especially the choir, I love your choir. I got goose pimples at one point.

E. F. (APOSTLE):   Who from, me?

TOOSIE: No, not from you, silly, from the choir. You should be proud of what you've done in such a short time.

E. F. (APOSTLE):   I quit school because I didn't like recess.

TOOSIE: Really?

E. F. (APOSTLE):   Well, the Lord has his own time clock and calendar. When you think of the millions and billions, trillions and quadrillions of years, even as there are stars in the sky, that the Lord has to work in, it's something that he would take the time to help with this holy little temple in such a wonderful way.

TOOSIE: That's a nice way to put it.

They sit and look and are aware of the immensity of the stars and the heavens above them.

TOOSIE *(continuing)*:   What on earth happened when you went out back with that nut?

E. F. (APOSTLE):   I'll never tell.

TOOSIE *(pulling on him and starting to laugh)*:   Come on, what happened? You must of been mad, because I sure know that I was mad when he started shouting at you, like he did.

E. F. (APOSTLE):   All I'll say is we didn't do no two-step, I can tell you that.

TOOSIE: I can see that; oh, you poor thing, with your black eye, look at you.

E. F. (APOSTLE):   No one is going to paralyze any dream of mine.

TOOSIE: What?

E. F. (APOSTLE):   What I said.

TOOSIE: I like the way you put that, say that again. *(pulling on him)*

E. F. (APOSTLE): Say what?

TOOSIE: What you just said.

E. F. (APOSTLE): It's true, there'll be no paralysis of an E. F. dream ever again, even if it takes a black eye or two somewhere along the way.

TOOSIE *(squeals)*: Listen to you.

E. F. (APOSTLE): It's true, whatever anybody may think about what I did out back there.

TOOSIE: Tell me something, what does E. F. stand for?

E. F. (APOSTLE): Why should I tell you?

TOOSIE: Because you should.

E. F. (APOSTLE) *(looks at her)*: It'll take another black eye before I tell you anything.

TOOSIE: Oh yeah?

E. F. (APOSTLE): Yeah.

TOOSIE *(she doubles up her fist and just looks at him)*: You're so intense sometimes, I love it!

She starts to hit at him. They laugh and wrestle around. We ...

CUT TO:

EXT. TOOSIE'S HOUSE—BUS—NIGHT

Pulling up and stopping.

E. F. (APOSTLE):   Well, here we go again.

TOOSIE *(look at each other)*:   What?

E. F. (APOSTLE):   At least tonight I'm gonna walk you to the front door.

TOOSIE: All right.

> *E. F. gets out and runs around to open her door as she giggles. They walk to her front door arm in arm. He casually takes her in his arms.*

E. F. (APOSTLE):   Well, darling.

TOOSIE: Yes.

E. F. (APOSTLE):   You think I'm intense, do you?

TOOSIE: A little, I like it.

E. F. (APOSTLE) *(looks at her)*:   Toosie—when I'm amongst people, I can fit in pretty well, always have. I can think about the Lord a lot, but I don't have to be always talking about him like most preachers. I feel pretty comfortable around you, I like you.

TOOSIE: I like you.

E. F. (APOSTLE):   Let me finish. When I get on the pulpit that's it. I go. And I know it's a bit foreign to you. I hope you'll accept me because in a way that's all that I am and all I got. If preaching is in any part of my body it's in my blood, and it'll be there until the day I die and go to Heaven, you hear me?

She nods. He kisses her strongly and passionately. He looks at her.

E. F. (APOSTLE) *(continuing)*: Come on, woman, come on!

He kisses her again.

TOOSIE *(she's overcome by it)*: What does E. F. stand for?

E. F. (APOSTLE): What do you want to know for?

TOOSIE: Because.

E. F. (APOSTLE): Let me come in and I'll tell you.

TOOSIE: Promise.

E. F. (APOSTLE): Yeah.

TOOSIE *(pause)*: Next time.

E. F. (APOSTLE): Next time? Maybe there won't even be a next time. I got to talk to you, Toosie. I got to talk to somebody. Please let me talk to you. Please.

TOOSIE: Next time.

E. F. lays one on her again. She loves it. She finally breaks and goes in.

TOOSIE *(continuing)*: I gotta go, you're too much.

As E. F. looks at her we . . .

CUT TO:

EXT. PHONE BOOTH—NIGHT

E. F. on the phone.

JOE *(V.O.)*:   You better come quick if you're gonna come. She's not doing well at all.

E. F. (APOSTLE):   Yeah, I'm gonna have to.

JOE *(V.O.)*:   They're looking for you more than ever. So I don't know. Think it over some.

CUT TO:

INT. MORTUARY—NIGHT

Joe facing an open casket. E. F.'s mother is lying on her back looking to heaven. As Joe sits and looks at the casket, we HEAR only his voice.

JOE *(V.O.)*:   I've been getting over to visit her most every day. She asks for you a lot. Sometimes she even thinks that I'm you and calls me Sonny.

E. F. (APOSTLE):   I'm gonna try to make it somehow. Tell her to hold on.

JOE *(V.O.)*:   I will, Brother. Although it may be too late. Be very, very careful whatever you do.

CUT TO:

INT. OFFICE—DAY

As E. F. passes Toosie's neatly laid out desk, he impulsively stops and scribbles her a note that he props

*up on a spot that she'll be sure to see as soon as she's
back at her desk.*

INT. ELMO'S OFFICE—DAY

*E. F. bounds up the stairs just as his little eight-man
choir starts singing an upbeat song over the air. He
sits by Brother Blackwell as they both smile and
beam at each other. As the choir sings we CUT. When
the singing stops we HEAR Elmo, V.O., asking for
tithes in order to keep "The Temple of the Living
God" alive and growing. "We are at a crucial period
with this fledgling church and we need your support
with dollars, checks, money orders, etc." V.O. continues over the following action.*

EXT. RURAL HOUSE—DAY

*CAMERA REVEALS Sam and E. F. sneaking a box-for-
the-needy up to the front door of a rural house. They
put the box down and run and hide under the foun-
dation after they have knocked loud and clear. They
are delighted when they hear voices, praising God in
gratitude, praising a latter-day miracle—the loaves
and the fishes in action in the twentieth century.*

EXT. CLUSTER OF HOMES—DAY

*As they stop by a cluster of homes, Sam goes one
way and E. F. peels off another way, each with a box
(in a WIDE SHOT). They put their respective boxes
down and, after they have knocked, they both run
for cover. Both parties come out simultaneously, see*

what they see and shout together, both praising God for the miracle from the Lord.

DISSOLVE TO:

EXT. STREET—DAY

It is mid-morning and the bus is broken down on its Sabbath day pick-up tour. The Apostle is standing in the street looking down at the flat left rear tire. There are several of his members around him surveying the situation. Most of the congregation—about twenty in all—have left the bus and are on the sidewalk. E. F. is a bit angry over the whole situation, but is doing a pretty fair job at covering.

E. F. (APOSTLE):   Sam, run over to that church over there and ask whoever is in charge to see if they can lend us a jack, if they have one.

Sam runs off in the direction of a rather large Catholic church that is short distance from where the bus is parked.

E. F. (APOSTLE) *(continuing; more to himself)*:   They must have a number of buses over there. *(he turns to a man nearby)* A spare tire without a jack is like a church without Jesus.

MAN SAYING 'AMEN':   Amen!

Sister Johnson (a very large woman) has stuck her head out and is looking to throw out any advice she can give.

SISTER JOHNSON: She's about as flat as she can be, ain't she?

E. F. (APOSTLE): You're right about that, Sister.

Sister Delilah sticks her head out and says:

SISTER DELILAH: Is this what you're looking for? *(she holds up a jack)*

E. F. (APOSTLE): Where on earth did you find that, Sister Delilah?

SISTER DELILAH: Under the backseat here; I was practically stepping on it.

E. F. (APOSTLE): Bless you, woman, gimme that thing.

He takes it and begins to adjust it.

SISTER DELILAH: The Lord's talking to me today. I'm gonna praise him this morning!

E. F. (APOSTLE): Amen, Sister, amen.

People have begun to gather around.

SISTER DELILAH: He's talking to me; he talks to me most all of the time.

SISTER JOHNSON: You probably never hear him half the time because you're always doing the talking. I don't hardly see how you have enough time to hear him when he does say something to you.

SISTER DELILAH: Sister Johnson, you better get off the bus now, because if you don't Papa E. F.'ll never get that thing pumped up enough to get the spare on. *(laughs at her own joke)*

SISTER JOHNSON: Why don't you offer the Apostle some of that cheap snuff you always stuffing behind your lower lip.

E. F. (APOSTLE):   Ladies, come on!

SISTER DELILAH: I ain't no cocaine addict like your son-in-law is. I don't take no dope, now do I?

The people laugh at the two ladies.

E. F. (APOSTLE):   Now, ladies, remember this is the Sabbath; and the Lord is not gonna take to all of this gossip and nit-pickin'!

SISTER DELILAH: I ain't saying nuthin'.

SISTER JOHNSON: You never do.

E. F. (APOSTLE):   Okay, ladies, off the bus, we're gonna jack this thing up now.

The ladies' heads disappear as E. F. starts to jack away.

At this moment Sam and a young PRIEST in a black gown appear. The priest has a jack in his hand.

PRIEST: Hello, will this help you?

E. F. (APOSTLE):   Thank you, sir, but we found our own, but God bless you for the gesture.

PRIEST: Well, I'm glad you're getting it fixed. What an awful thing to have happen. Where are you located, your church?

E. F. (APOSTLE): We're at 4012 South 4th Street. We're only a small temple, nuthing like your all's, but we're growing.

PRIEST: So I've heard—That's good, just so you don't take too many of ours with you.

E. F. (APOSTLE): You wouldn't miss just a few now would you?

PRIEST *(laughing)*: I don't like losing even one.

E. F. (APOSTLE): I tell you, even if I ended up running off with about fifteen or twenty of your people—and you never know—that still leaves you a good balance or the better part of about seven hundred million, don't it?

PRIEST: Well, I suppose so. *(laughs)* You say you're over on South 4th Street?

E. F. (APOSTLE): Yes, sir—come on over sometime. Everybody's welcome.

PRIEST: Thank you.

E. F. (APOSTLE): You ever been in a Holiness church?

PRIEST: I don't believe I have.

E. F. (APOSTLE): Come on over. I guarantee we don't sit on our hands.

SISTER DELILAH: Amen.

Others say "Praise God."

E. F. (APOSTLE):   You might enjoy it.

PRIEST: I'm sure I would, thank you. Maybe I'll take you up on that. I better get back. Do you need anything else?

E. F. (APOSTLE):   No, sir, we appreciate your kindness, God bless you.

PRIEST: Have a good day.

He leaves as others thank him as well.

E. F. (APOSTLE):   Adios, Padre.

DISSOLVE TO:

INT. BUS—DAY

Everybody getting back on the bus. E. F. starts up the motor.

MAN SAYING 'AMEN':   We won't be too late, will we?

E. F. (APOSTLE):   How can we be when we're it?

MAN SAYING 'AMEN':   It's already 11:15.

E. F. (APOSTLE):   Why don't we start church right here on the bus, that way we can't be late. Somebody say we're going to have church on the move.

They yell it again.

E. F. starts up the singing and a few others join in.

PEOPLE: Come on! Amen.

*Then the choir members and everyone else join in.
Soon the whole bus is rocking in song. Sister Delilah
gets up and begins dancing in the Spirit in the center
aisle. There is much hand clapping and good fellowship. The Spirit is there!!*

CUT TO:

EXT. BUS—DAY

A WIDE EXTERIOR SHOT

*Of the little bus rolling along with the Catholic
Church disappearing in the background. We HEAR
the singing over the bus as it heads for the "Temple
of the Living God."*

DISSOLVE TO:

EXT. AUCTION—DAY

A CAKE AUCTION

*Going on. Balloons are being handed out with a
homemade banner reading: "Balloon Sunday for Our
Young." Elmo broadcasts a live play-by-play account
of the activities via a portable microphone. As
Brother Blackwell observes the festivities, we FOL-
LOW his eyes to the following:*

*The Troublemaker that the Apostle whipped on
Wednesday evening is driving up on a bulldozer. He
has several of his friends and relatives alongside of*

him. The Apostle sees them and moves over to confront them.

The Apostle steps up.

E. F. (APOSTLE):   We could've used you for a bit of bus transportation this morning. Welcome.

TROUBLEMAKER: I told you I'd be back.

E. F. (APOSTLE):   Yes, sir, I believe you did at that.

At this point a patrol car passes by, slowing down only a bit and then cruising on down the street and out of view. Members of both groups are aware of this.

E. F. (APOSTLE) *(continuing)*:   Would you gentlemen care to join in the bidding for some pretty fair homemade cakes and pies?

TROUBLEMAKER *(moves bulldozer closer)*:   I'm not here for that purpose, Apostle.

E. F. (APOSTLE):   What are you here for then, cowboy?

TROUBLEMAKER: Step out of the way, Apostle. I'm gonna take your church out of there. We don't want it here no more.

E. F. (APOSTLE):   But the Lord wants it to stay right on that spot where I'm pointing.

TROUBLEMAKER: But we don't want it here. Just step aside.

CUT TO:

BLACKWELL AND CROWD

TROUBLEMAKER: Send the children on down the street. We don't want them to get scared.

E. F. (APOSTLE):   Nobody's going anywheres, and this House of God stays right where it's at.

TROUBLEMAKER: Step aside, I said.

E. F. (APOSTLE):   I ain't gonna whip you, mister. I did that the other night. I'm not gonna whip you, but the Lord will.

TROUBLEMAKER: Step aside.

E. F. opens Bible to the 91st Psalm and lays it on the ground directly in front of the bulldozer. E. F. steps aside. E. F. quotes a very apropos verse from the Bible and tells the man to proceed. Man looks at him and the Bible as he guns his motor.

E. F. (APOSTLE):   You touch that church you gotta go over that Holy Book and, Brother, when you do, I don't want to be sittin' where you're sittin' right now . . .

TROUBLEMAKER *(intense)*:   Move that Bible.

E. F. (APOSTLE):   . . . 'cause he's gonna strike you down like you've never been struck, that's a promise I can make you on this Sunday morning. It's up to you.

TROUBLEMAKER: Move it.

E. F. (APOSTLE):   No, sir, you can move against the Lord if you so desire. I have nuthin' to do with it anymore.

*The Troublemaker's friends look at him. The Trouble-
maker feels uncomfortable as he looks at them and
then looks to E. F. the Apostle, who holds his gaze.*

CUT TO:

THE CROWD

Comments from them.

CUT TO:

WIDE SHOT

*The Troublemaker gets off his bulldozer and goes
over to pick up the Bible. Nobody moves. The man
gets on one knee to pick up the Bible. He just stays
there for a moment. He covers his face, concealing
great shame and other emotions. He begins to ask for
forgiveness. As he speaks out loud with remorse and
humility, the Apostle goes to him and kneels with
him. The Troublemaker asks if E. F. will forgive him.*

E. F. (APOSTLE):   All the way, Brother.

TROUBLEMAKER: Thank you.

E. F. (APOSTLE):   You bet, and I'll kneel with you.

TROUBLEMAKER: I don't want to knock your church over.

E. F. (APOSTLE):   I know you don't, neighbor, and I'm
gonna pray with you and I'll cry with you if you want
me to.

TROUBLEMAKER: Will the Lord forgive me?

E. F. (APOSTLE):   You'll have to ask him; only he can tell
you that. I have no such power, my friend. Reach
out to him and he'll accept you at this very moment.

*E. F. takes the Troublemaker's hand and places it on
the Bible. As the man asks forgiveness, he accepts
Jesus Christ.*

E. F. (APOSTLE) *(continuing)*:   He is your Lord here today
and he will be your Lord forever more. He loves you
just as each and every one of us here loves you. Now
let's praise Him.

DISSOLVE TO:

EXT. GRAVE SITE—NIGHT

*We see a figure crawling through the woods to a
gravestone. CAMERA pans left to a police car, where
we find an OFFICER sleeping. We pan back to the
figure as it reaches the gravestone. A hand reaches
out and touches the grave.*

E. F. (APOSTLE):   Good-bye, Momma. I love you and I'll
meet you in Heaven.

*As E. F. crawls away, we pan back to the police car
as the officer stirs. When we pan back to the crawling
figure, nobody is there.*

INT. KITCHEN—RESTAURANT—DAY

*The Apostle is working in the kitchen of a restaurant
as a short order cook. He takes two orders and places*

them on his rotating piece of equipment. He then picks up two plates and puts them on a counter framed by an open square area. The waitress, TERRY, on the other side takes the order away to her two customers. HELPER is listening to a tape of E. F. preaching on the radio. E. F. turns the dial; the helper turns it back.

HELPER: Doesn't working here tire you out for preaching?

E. F. (APOSTLE):   Well, I can only work part-time. I do get tired but the Lord always gives me the energy if I need it and when I need it!

HELPER: You got a lot more than I do, I can tell you that.

E. F. (APOSTLE):   It's not me, Brother. Praise God! It's the Lord working through me!

He looks out the little window and after his eyes focus he just stares, quietly.

CUT TO:

WHAT HE SEES

He sees Toosie, two BOYS, and an adult MAN. They are sitting down at a table right in his line of vision. As they order, they chatter and talk with one another and Toosie reaches casually over and brushes the hair back on one of the boys. Automatically, E. F. takes his apron and hat off and lays them to one side.

He is about to walk out when Terry comes back with Toosie and her family's order.

He looks at them and begins to prepare their meal.

DISSOLVE TO:

E. F.

Putting the four plates down for the waitress to pick up. He rings the bell and as she is about to pick them up, E. F. says:

E. F. (APOSTLE):   Terry, tell the boss I quit, these are my last four orders.

TERRY: Really.

E. F. (APOSTLE):   That's it. Really.

He takes two steps backward and frames the serving area in his hands.

E. F.   (APOSTLE) *(continuing)*:   I'll never serve nuthin' through that window again. That's it! Never again.

TERRY *(looks at him puzzled)*:   I'll tell him.

E. F. turns around and walks out. His helper calls after him, "Where you going?"

E. F. (APOSTLE):   I'm going for a walk!

CUT TO:

EXT. POLICE STATION—DAY

E. F. walking up to a police station and just looking. As he is about to enter, he changes his mind and sits on a side step, just staring; he whistles to a dog, who looks at him and keeps on going. As he looks back at the entrance we HOLD and ...

CUT TO:

INT. TEMPLE—DAY

REVEAL SAM

Approaching a back room in the temple. He slows down as he hears voices. He stops outside of a doorway and just listens. The CAMERA FLOATS around the corner and REVEALS E. F. and Brother Blackwell in a TWO SHOT talking. The Apostle is confessing his crime to his friend and co-pastor.

E. F. (Apostle):   That's why I preach different on radio, that's why I'm a mystery, that's why I came out of nowhere out of the blue. And being here may be the best thing I've ever done in my life.

Blackwell: What do you want to do?

E. F. (Apostle):   What do you want me to do?

Blackwell: Whatever you want; we love you and you've helped many, many people in the town.

Sam listening.

E. F. (Apostle):   I'm gonna stay for now.

Blackwell: The Lord will decide and dictate how long you should be here. It's His will.

E. F. (APOSTLE):   Take my gold, my watch, hock 'em, get use of every penny we can get and save to help keep the ministry going, 'cause I don't know how long the Lord will let me be with you.

BLACKWELL: We'll all know. He places us right where he wants us at all times and in all places. Do you believe that?

E. F. (APOSTLE):   Amen, Brother, I do.

HOLD ON SAM

As he tiptoes away with his hands covering his ears.

DISSOLVE TO:

INT. JESSIE'S CAR—DAY

A WOMAN'S HAND ON A CAR RADIO

As it reaches down and tries to clear the station of the static that is mixed with the voice. As the hand turns the volume up, we can HEAR the Apostle imitating the style and content of his deceased grandfather's speech. The CAMERA WIDENS and we SEE that the woman listening is the Apostle's estranged wife, Jessie, three hundred miles away in Fort Worth, Texas.

E.F. (APOSTLE):   Any lovely lady would love to wear one of these beautiful scarves. For just seven dollars and ninety-five cents you can receive one of these beautifully hand-painted scarves here in Pecan Isl—

Here the static completely blots out the voice on the other end.

Jessie looks puzzled but somewhat enlightened as she speeds on her way home. We . . .

CUT TO:

INT. RADIO STATION—DAY

The Apostle is finishing his scarf routine as the CAMERA COMES UP on him and Elmo in the broadcasting room. Elmo takes over and begins giving the particulars once again to the audience out in radio land. He tells them that the radio ministry is really beginning to roll.

INT. GARAGE/RADIO STATION—DAY

During Elmo's speech Toosie comes in and sees a funny-looking heart-shaped doll with two extending fists. On the heart is written, "I love you this much." She looks at it and then puts it way in the back drawer of her desk so nobody will see it. She then exits.

INT. ELMO'S OFFICE—DAY

ELMO: We have gained more momentum and even more momentum in our drive to sustain not only our station—and we have expanded and do intend to expand to even more counties in Louisiana and Texas—but we have put some of these generous tithes into the One-Way Road to Heaven Holiness Temple right here in downtown Pecan Island.

During Elmo's speech the CAMERA BEGINS TO COME IN on E. F., who seems quiet and somewhat detached, staring straight ahead. As we HOLD on him, we . . .

CUT TO:

INT. TEMPLE—NIGHT

E. F. is conducting a midweek testimonial meeting.

E. F. (APOSTLE):   We'll need to have a Baby Jesus. So anybody who has a volunteer, let us know, otherwise we could always use a doll of some type. Those who want to be wise men, you all sign up with Mother Blackwell. She's gonna be doing the directing of the Christmas pageant, most of it anyhow, because I know I don't know much about that kind of thing. Any country people who want to donate any animals, goats, lambs, whatever, that would be greatly appreciated. We only got three weeks or more, so we have to get on it. Also, after the first of the year, we're going to start a marriage workshop. Brother Blackwell will preside; he definitely is more successful than I ever was at any time in my experience. If Las Vegas can build casinos that tear marriages apart, can't we build a modest temple that saves marriages and salvages them? Right, Brother Blackwell?

BLACKWELL: Yes, sir, we're gonna give it a try.

E. F. (APOSTLE):   Hallelujah! No tag-team parenthood!

E. F. notices a STATE TROOPER standing in the back of the church.

E. F. (Apostle) *(continuing):*   Sit down, Brother, and we'll be with you after the service. You can benefit from this, so just sit tight for a while.

Sister Delilah pops up and starts to testify. E. F. looks as if he might want to stop her but doesn't.

Sister Delilah: I was married twice and both my husbands were good Christians, but they've both gone on; I don't want no more husbands, but I do want to participate in Brother Blackwell's workshops—

Sister Johnson gives her a look.

Sister Delilah *(continuing):*   —maybe, the Lord willing, I could offer some of my experience to help others, because I loved my two husbands and now they've gone on, but God is leading me now and I don't need nobody; praise God for Jesus, he's by my side now!

As she sits, E. F. says:

E. F. (Apostle):   I think it would be appropriate if George plays for us. He's been practicing and I think it's time now. Let's give a big handclap for George. He's gonna play, what is it?

George *(mumbles):*   "Had It Not Been."

E. F. (Apostle):   "Had It Not Been"—Thank you, George, God bless you!

The old black man gets up out of the first row and goes up to the pulpit, readies himself, and begins to play his cornet. As he does, E. F. goes into the back office of the church to use the telephone. The state trooper keeps his eye directly on the spot when he exits. E. F. can see back over the cornet player onto the congregation. He dials and waits. We . . .

CUT TO:

INT. BEDROOM—NIGHT

JESSIE

On the other end. He waits, as does she. We INTER-CUT. Finally . . .

JESSIE: Sonny.

E. F. (APOSTLE): I'd like to speak to my beauties.

Pause.

JESSIE: Where are you, Sonny?

E. F. (APOSTLE): Is Bobby and Jess there?

JESSIE: No! I'm going to pray for you, because you're a murderer. I'm going to pray for you even if it will do no good.

E. F. (APOSTLE): Pray with me, Momma, not at me. Pray with me.

CUT TO:

INT. TEMPLE—NIGHT

THE PRESENT

We FIND the Apostle E. F. preaching his last sermon to his fledgling congregation. As he preaches he stops every now and again, and says, "Stay with me now," and "Are you still here, say amen. Hello!"

NOTE: During the entire final sermon, we intercut scenes from E. F.'s life:

EXT. TOOSIE'S HOUSE—DAY

Toosie playing touch football with her kids and husband.

INT. HOSPITAL—DAY

The final moments of Horace's life in the hospital.

EXT. RIVERBANK—BAYOU—DAY

The Old Bayou Man at the bayou.

EXT. TEMPLE—DAY

Police car waiting outside.

INT. MORTUARY—NIGHT

Jessie and the two kids in front of their grandmother's coffin.

INT. BAR—DAY

Joe sitting in a bar drinking.

INT. ROOM—DAY

Man from the car crash in the opening with his wife and newborn baby.

INT. MORTUARY—DAY

Mother Dewey climbing into her own coffin and assuming the death position.

INT. ELMO'S OFFICE—DAY

Elmo at the radio station playing and singing a rock-and-roll song.

INT. TEMPLE—DAY

E. F. (APOSTLE):   You have to work at it. But anyone who dedicates his life to Christ is a saint.

The congregation praises God; one woman speaks in tongues.

He tells them salvation is free, but not cheap.

E. F. (APOSTLE) *(continuing)*:   Learn your ABCs. A—Acknowledge that you are a sinner. B—Believe in Jesus Christ, trust in Him. C—Confess that you are saved. Confess it to others, shout it in the hills and valleys!

If you keep your eye on Jesus, he will keep his eye on you, just as you can't escape the gaze of a painted picture on the wall. No matter where you look its eyes will follow you as will the eyes of Jesus Christ. Withersoever Thou leadest, I will follow and 'Lo, I am with you always. Everybody say always. Monday, Tuesday, Wednesday, Thursday, Friday, Saturday, Sunday—twenty-four hours a day, seven days a week. When you turn, He turns, when I jump up and down, Jesus jumps up and down and, neighbor, He backs up what I'm preaching here tonight. Somebody give me an Amen! He's backing me up tonight. You grab somebody, look 'em in the eyeballs, and say, Jesus, He's here right now! Jesus, the same yesterday, today and forever! Anytime you think the Devil is getting ahead of you, you say, "Get thou behind me, Satan." Somebody say Get! Get behind me, old Slew Foot, because the Lord don't want me drinking because He's got his eye on me. You can't hide the bottle if He's got his eye on you. Get behind me because the Lord don't want me to go out dancing, He's got his eye on me. Get behind me because the Lord don't want me sinning, He's got his eye on me. Hello, are you still there? The Lord has his everlasting eye on me and you, because He loves you and me and why does He love us, how do we know that He loves us here tonight? How do we know He'll love us from now until the end of eternity, how do we know that? Because He sent his only begotten Son into the world and put him in a tabernacle of clay so that we could recognize Him. He came to save us. He could have called on ten thousand angels, but He had to take our place, He hung on that tree so we wouldn't have to! That cruel, cruel tree. He died for us so that we could be saved, and we can be saved free of charge, but it ain't cheap. Am I right this evening? You have to pay an earthly price, but I tell you it's worth it, it's worth it here tonight! If He sent his only begotten Son, put him in a tabernacle or recognizable clay and then arose him up from the grave to atone for our sins, don't you think it would be worthwhile to just examine somewhat what He might be askin' for in return, an examination of what is put out there for us free, not cheap, but free. It was paid for nineteen hundred years ago! Do you want it, then you can have it, you can be saved—I know I want it and once you've felt even three or four hundred volts of the Holy Spirit, then I know you're gonna want it. Do you want to get plugged in? Come on!!! Do I hear somebody say Amen? You might get three in one, the Father, Son, and the Holy Ghost, that's a mighty high-charged baptism; if you want it, be saved, and go for it. If God sent his only Son then it's worth the price—Are you on the Devil's Hit List?—Put all these elements of the Devil behind you, work on it, put all the combined satanic forces behind you and get right with God here tonight. This ain't no petty subject, this is Holy Ghost power we're talking about. Get that Holy Ghost explosion tonight, we gonna short-circuit the Devil. We gonna put him behind us. You Devil stay there, you hear? My—my—my—we're gonna be with Jesus tonight. Everybody say it. Say it again! Let all the other churches in Pecan Island hear you and one more time!

E. F. goes into the audience and picks up a little BABY BOY out of the arms of one of his parishioners. The WOMAN is Vietnamese, as is her baby. Holding the child's tiny hand up in his—

E. F. (APOSTLE) *(continuing)*: Look at these beautiful, beautiful little hands; now try to imagine a nail, piercing the palms of this child's hands and then picture the nail going into an old board. I know I don't have enough love in my heart to do this to my son, do you? I know I know I don't! I don't have that much love in me, but God does, God does. *(as he hands the baby back, he says)* Bless you. Put your hand over your heart and with the other hand reach out and touch somebody. The Holy Ghost can and will enter you. But there is yet another side to this issue. On the other side of the Holy Ghost explosion is a still small voice, the still small voice of Jesus within you, in your heart, talking to you, leading you. This powerful quiet force can reach to the darkest part of Africa, it can penetrate the most calloused and hard-hearted atheist you'd ever want to meet! The voice of Jesus Christ can reach into any place in the universe where there's a willing and open heart! The only place the still and small voice of Jesus Christ cannot enter is into the heart of any man or woman who says "No, you cannot come in." *(touches a YOUNG BOY)* "You cannot enter here tonight." *(pause)* Neighbor, someday I'm gonna sit with Jesus. I was going to help my grandfather preach the Holy Gospel. If I hadn't come back to help my granddad, I could be there tonight. I could be there in Heaven tonight with Jesus, even as I know I will be again someday, as I hope and pray to the almighty God that each and every one of you blessed people will be there someday, when we shall all be promoted as soldiers of Jesus into eternal and liquid Glory, somebody give it to me, let the Church say Amen! *(he stands and says)* Is there anyone who wants to accept our Lord and Saviour Jesus Christ as his personal Saviour, let him come forward. Can you say I am sitting flat on ready tonight! For any mother's son or daughter who wants it! It's here tonight, Jesus is here! It's time, the Holy Ghost Conductor is calling, "All aboard, all aboard!"

(As he opens his arms in an extended welcome, he sings "Just As I Am" or "Softly and Tenderly.") He waits for some time before it is Sam that comes forward. E. F. is very touched as he welcomes Sam and tells him "His heart is broke for joy tonight." He speaks lovingly and like a father into Sam's ear at the altar and tells him in St. Paul's words, "Any man who is saved is a saint." People gather around Sam and help. A little girl dabs her eyes with a handkerchief.

E. F. (APOSTLE) (continuing): You're going to Heaven. *(and to himself)* And I'm going to jail.

He stands and looks at the State Trooper.

E. F. (APOSTLE) *(continuing)*: How many believe I preached today?

b his guitar player and then to the choir.
s at the piano.)

continuing): I'm gonna leave you now.
Let's have the choir come up here and give us an
old joyous hymn of Pentecost. Come on, come on!
Satan has called me to the arena one more time!

*He puts his microphone up as the choir files up and
forms in front of the pulpit. They begin to sing as the
white guitar player and a LARGE BLACK WOMAN
lead them. People walk in the spirit—two or three
dance.*

*The Apostle steps down and kisses a SMALL CHILD
good-bye. He passes through the congregation and
walks to the State Trooper, who stands and waits for
him. He notices a LITTLE BLACK BOY trying to help
a LITTLE WHITE BOY catch the rhythm of the beat
as they clap.*

*He looks back at his friend Brother Blackwell; for a
moment he wonders if it was the brother who be-
trayed him. He turns and walks out of the church
with the State Trooper. Sam follows him out and
goes up to the police car behind the Apostle.*

EXT. TEMPLE—NIGHT

STATE TROOPER: Are you Euliss Dewey?

E. F. (APOSTLE): I'm the Apostle E. F.

STATE TROOPER: We'd like to ask you some questions about a homicide up in Fort Worth.

E. F. (APOSTLE): Who was killed?

STATE TROOPER: Are you Euliss F. Dewey?

E. F. (APOSTLE): I've been known by a lot of names, officer. *(he turns)* Sam, you go on back now, you hear, go back inside, where you're needed.

Sam looks at him, turns around and goes back to the front door of the Temple.

STATE TROOPER: We'd like for you to come with us for some routine questioning.

E. F. (APOSTLE): Yes, sir.

WIDE SHOT of church and E. F. getting into the police car.

STATE TROOPER: You are Euliss F. Dewey, aren't you?

E. F. (APOSTLE): Yes, sir, I was; I'm an Apostle for our Lord now. I'm the man you're looking for.

INT. POLICE CAR—NIGHT

As they drive away:

E. F. (APOSTLE): I thought you fellows quit driving these Chevys. I thought you switched to Fords like they've done back in Texas.

All the while the choir can be heard singing a wonderful old hymn: "Jesus, He's All Right." We . . .

CUT TO:

EXT. ROAD—DAY

THE CLOSING SEQUENCE

As the CREDITS start to roll, we SEE a CHAIN GANG OF PRISONERS. We HEAR the Apostle preaching. We SEE him for the last time—a little older—as he administers to the needy.

The voices of the choir continue throughout the CLOSING CREDITS.

Credits and Cast List

OCTOBER FILMS PRESENTS

A BUTCHERS RUN FILMS PRODUCTION

A ROBERT DUVALL Film

THE APOSTLE

Robert Duvall
Farrah Fawcett
Todd Allen
John Beasley
June Carter Cash
Walton Goggins
Billy Joe Shaver
Billy Bob Thornton
and Miranda Richardson

Casting	RENEE ROUSSELOT
	ED JOHNSTON
Costume Designer	DOUGLAS HALL
Music Supervisor	PETER AFTERMAN
Original Score	DAVID MANSFIELD

Co-Producer	**STEVEN BROWN**
Editor	**STEPHEN MACK**
Production Designer	**LINDA BURTON**
Director of Photography	**BARRY MARKOWITZ**
Executive Producer	**ROBERT DUVALL**
Producer	**ROB CARLINER**
Written and Directed by	**ROBERT DUVALL**

CAST
(In Alphabetical Order)

Horace	**TODD ALLEN**
Tag Team Preacher #3	**BROTHER PAUL BAGGET**
Female Sonny Supporter	**LENORE BANKS**
Brother Blackwell	**JOHN BEASLEY**
Mother Blackwell	**MARY LYNETTE BRAXTON**
Helper	**BRETT BROCK**
Sister Johnson's Twins	**CHRISTOPHER & CHRISTIAN CANADY**
Mrs. Dewey, Sr.	**JUNE CARTER CASH**
Singer	**ELIZABETH CHISOLM**
Bayou Man	**BROTHER WILLIAM ATLAS COLE**

Soloist #4	REVEREND FRANK COLLINS, JR.
Civic Auditorium Preacher	PROPHET CARL D. COOK
Scripture Reader	NAOMI CRAIG
Liquor Store Preacher	WAYNE DEHART
Elmo	RICK DIAL
The Apostle E.F.	ROBERT DUVALL
Jessie Dewey	FARRAH FAWCETT
Needy Receiver #2	JAN FAWCETT
Young Priest	JAMES IVEY GLEASON
Sam	WALTON GOGGINS
Tag Team Preacher #5	REVEREND CHILI GRAHAM
Tag Team Preacher #1	REVEREND BOBBY GREEN
Texas State Trooper	STUART GREER
Sonny Supporter #1	JOHN E. HAWKINS
Child Accordionist	HUNTER HAYES
Flashback Preacher	REVEREND DANIEL HICKMAN
Virgil	EMERY HOPKINS
Faith Healer #2	BRENDA B. JACKSON
Sister Jewell	SISTER JEWELL JERNIGAN
Tag Team Preacher #2	REVEREND CHARLES JOHNSON
Baptism Soloist	JULIE JOHNSON
Faith Healer #1	VERA KEMP
Soloist #1	JOSEPH LINDSEY
Church Woman	SHARON K. LONDON
Sister Johnson	ZELMA LOYD
Doctor	FERNIE E. MCMILLAN
Church Member #2	JIMMIE J. MEAUX
Bodyguard	L. CHRISTIAN MIXON
Church Man #2	RICHARD NANCE
Louisiana State Trooper	DOUGLAS PERRY

Coronet George	**HAROLD POTIER, SR.**
Young Man in Car	**KEVIN RANKIN**
Accident Witness	**PAT RATLIFF**
Toosie	**MIRANDA RICHARDSON**
Sonny at 12 years old	**JAY ROBICHEAUX**
Man Saying "Amen"	**TERENCE ROSEMORE**
Joe	**BILLY JOE SHAVER**
Sister Delilah	**JOYCE JOLIVET STARKS**
Jessie Jr.	**CHRISTINA STOJANOVICH**
Bobbie	**NICHOLAS STOJANOVICH**
Needy Receiver	**RONNIE STUTES**
Soloist/Choir Director	**RUBY FRANCIS TERRY**
Troublemaker	**BILLY BOB THORNTON**
Church Man #1	**GRAHAM TIMBES**
Nosey Neighbor	**JAMES B. TOWRY**
Latin Translator	**RENEE VICTOR**
Sonny Supporter #2	**REVEREND JESSE WALDROP**
Tag Team Preacher #4	**REVEREND STEVE WHITE**
Tag Team Preacher #5	**SISTER FAY WINN**
Soloist #3	**MELETE WOODS**

**Fountain of the Living Word Church
of Dallas, Texas, Choir**

MARGARET OLIVER	
COLEMAN	**SHARON DENISE DICKERSON**
ERICA LYNN DUNCAN	**SONDRA JACKSON GREEN**
DAVID HENDERSON	**PARLA J. JOHNSON**
DONNA SIDDIQUI	**TAMI BOAZ SKELTON**
RACHEL V. STEVENSON	**GRETCHEN LOUISE WATTS**

Organist	**JERRY H. SKELTON, PASTOR**

Mr. Duvall's Stunt Double   MARK DE ALESSANDRO

Crew

Associate Producer	ED JOHNSTON
Unit Production Manager	TAYLOR FAVALE
First Assistant Director	LOUIS SHAW MILITO
Second Assistant Director	CHAD ROSEN
Post Production Supervisor	SHARRE JACOBY
Camera Operator	BARRY MARKOWITZ
First Assistant Camera	STEVEN SEARCH
Second Assistant Camera	EHAB ASAL
	NICK FRANCO
"B" Camera/SteadiCam Operator	JERRY HOLWAY
Loader	SHANE WEAVER
Still Photographer	Van Redin
2nd Second Assistant Director	MELISSA CUMMINS LORENZ
Script Supervisors	CAROL BANKER
	MAIME MITCHELL
Sound Mixer	STEVE C. AARON, C.A.S.
Boom Operator	RANDY PEASE
Assistant Editor	FULVIO VALSANGIACOMO
Art Director	IRFAN AKDAG

Art Department Coordinator	SHELLY C. STOLL
Set Decorators	LORI JOHNSON
	DEA JENSEN
Property Master	SAMUEL J. TELL
Property Assistants	GERT BROEKEMA
	NATHAN BONISKE
Leadman	KEN-E-RAY RECTOR
Set Dresser	DEBORAH DAWSON
Swing	JEAN-PAUL GUIRARD
	JON JENKINS
Scenics	NAN PARATI
	TOM DAVIS
On-Set Dresser	ALEXANDRA TAGER
Costume Supervisor	LISA PARMET
Costumers	MEREDITH MCLAUGHLIN
	ANGELA NUÑEZ
	SUSAN THOMAS
Cutter/Fitter	JANIE BARGARON
Key Makeup Artists	ALLISON GORDIN
	LILY GART
Key Hairstylist	ALICIA DOLLARD
Ms. Fawcett's Makeup and Hair	MELA MURPHY
Stunt Coordinator	ETHAN JENSEN
Gaffer	JOHN WAGNER
Best Boy	BEAR E. SMITH

Electricians	PAUL D. BEARD
	DARRIN DICKERSON
	ROCKY "ROCKMAN" FORD
	DENNIS NOY HADEN
	KEVIN LONG
	DAVID TAYLOR
Cable Puller	R. FRANK KINCEL II
Key Grip	TOM GRUNKE
Best Boy	SCOTT S. FAWLEY
Dolly Grip	MIKE DUNSON
Grips	GORDON ARD
	TODD DAVIS
	RANDY GALLAGHER
	STEPHEN RITCHEY
	STEVEN LYNN WALKER
	DON W. WEGNER
Video Playback	SAMONE BENNETT
Location Coordinator/ Scout	STEPHANIE SAMUEL DUPUY
Location Manager/Scout	VIRGINIA MCCOLLAM
Location Manager	PETER WILSON
Location Assistants	ASHLEY HASPEL
	GREG GUIRARD
Dialect Coaches	ELIZABETH HIMELSTEIN
	FRANCIE BROWN
Production Accountant	DESIRÉE KILLIAN
Assistant Production Accountant	STACEY BALLENTINE
Production Coordinator	ONNI VOSDOGANES

Assistant Production	ADAM PRINCE
Coordinators	CHRISTI ALEXANDER
Extras Casting	TANYA SULLIVAN
Casting Assistant	JAMI RUDOFSKY
Extras Casting Assistants	TONI COBB BROCK
	LISA W. SUIRE
Craft Service	NANCY JAMES
	RHONDA BYERS LEE
Construction Coordinator	JOHN N. PATTERSON
Construction Foreman	JAMES DUPUY
Carpenter	HUEY MITCHELL
	BILL DARROW
Transportation Coordinator	LAWRENCE MORGAN
Transportation Captain	AARON C. WINCE
Honeywagon Driver	NICK PASTRANO
Production Van Driver	FRED POPE JR.
Drivers	JAMES CEDOTAL
	MARK EVANS
	ROOSTER LAYTON
	ISRAEL MARTIN
	MARK MEAUX
	SONNY MESSINA
	L. CHRISTIAN MIXON
	LUKE MORRIS
	CHRISTIE NEZAT
	LINDA NITSCH
	DAVID "PETE" PETERSON
	ALBERT J. SPARKS JR.
	BOBBY WILLIAMSON

Catering	**LOCATION CATERING SERVICES**

Production Assistants	**LESLIE BOURQUE**
	ANDREW EVANS
	SHELBY HYMAN
	NATASHA SANCHEZ
	EDWIN VONSCHONDORF
Film Runner	**ERIC BARKER**

Set Medic	**SHELLY KUJAWA**
Set Teacher	**JOEL T. BIBLE**
Security	**CHARLES W. ANDERS SECURITY SERVICES**
Mr. Duvall's Stand-in	**RONALD STUTES**
Mrs. Carter Cash's Stand-in	**JUDY HARRINGTON**
Ms. Fawcett's Stand-in	**JAN FAWCETT**
Mr. Shaver's Stand-in	**CHARLES WHITE**
Utility Stand-in	**MICHAEL HACKNEY**

LAFAYETTE CHILDREN'S CHOIR
CHILDREN'S CHOIR DIRECTOR ELI WILSON
SUNBEAM CHOIR
THE APOSTLE CHURCH CHOIR
CHOIR AT SONNY'S TEMPLE
THE SW LOUISIANA MASS CHOIR

Supervising Sound Editor	**JOHN NUTT**

Supervising Rerecordist	**MARK BERGER**
Recordist	**DAVID PARKER**

Sound Effects Editors	**KYRSTEN MATE COMOGLIO**
	MALCOLM FIFE
Assistant Sound Editors	**TOBIN JOHN DELACCA DAVIS**
	YIN DODD
Apprentice Sound Editor	**CASEY NUTT**
Foley Artists	**MARNIE MOORE**
	LESLIE BLOOME
Foley Mixers	**STEPHEN HART**
	STEVEN FONTANO
	FRANK RINELLA
ADR Services	**BRIAN RUBERG**
	TODD-AO STUDIOS
ADR Voice Casting	**BARBARA HARRIS**
Machine Room Supervisor	**FRANK CANONICA**
Machine Room Operators	**ANNA GEYER**
	LOREN BYER
	GRANT FOERSTER
Transfer Supervisor	**JEFF WHITTLE**
Transfer Operator	**RICK KAHN**
Sound Post-Production Services	**SAUL ZAENTZ FILM CENTER**

Mixed at **SAUL ZAENTZ FILM CENTER**

Main and End Titles Designed by	**NINA SAXON FILM DESIGN**
Typesetting by	**SCARLET LETTERS**
	BEN SCHOEN

Opticals and Titles by   HOWARD ANDERSON, INC.
Optical Supervisor   JEFF HUTCHISON
Dailies and Telecine
Transfers   CFI
Color Timer   DAN MUSCARELLA
Lok-Box Negative Cutting   GLENN SUFFERN

Musical Score Performed by
DAVID MANSFIELD

Associate Music Supervisor
ELIZABETH WENDEL

Music Editor   SHARON SMITH
Assistant to Music Supervisor MARGARET YEN
Score Engineered by   DAN GELLERT
Music Mixed at   AVATAR STUDIOS

SONGS
"What Passes for Love"
Written by David Grissom
Performed by Storyville
Courtesy of Atlantic Recording Corp.
By Arrangement with Warner Special Products

"There Ain't No Grave (Gonna Hold My Body Down)"
Written by Claude Ely
Performed by Robert Duvall

"Waitin' on the Far Side Banks of Jordan"
Written by Terry Smith
Performed by June Carter Cash

"Handwriting on the Wall"
Written by Mel Mallory
Performed by Little Leo
Courtesy of Tuff City/Night Train International Records
By Arrangement with Ocean Park Music Group

"Eunice Waltz"
Written by Floyd Soileau, Maurice Berzas
Performed by Steve Riley and the Marnou Playboys

"The Bible Rap Song"
Written by Eli Wilson, Cathy Johnson, Cornela Jones

"Bayou Pon Pon"
Arranged by D. L. Menard, Eddie Lejeune, Ken Smith
Performed by Le Trio Cadien
Courtesy of Rounder Records
By Arrangement with Ocean Park Music Group

"What's It All About"
Written by Mel Mallory
Performed by Little Leo
Courtesy of Tuff City/Night Train International Records
By Arrangement with Ocean Park Music Group

"You Didn't Have to Say It, Out Loud"
Written by Randy Sharp, Chris Farren
Performed by Chris Farren
Courtesy of Windswept Pacific Entertainment Co.

"I'll Fly Away"
Written by Albert E. Brumley

Performed by The Fountain of the Living Word Church of
Dallas, Texas, Choir

"Two Coats"
Performed by Patty Loveless

"I Will Not Go Quietly"
Written by Steven Curtis Chapman
Performed by Steven Curtis Chapman

"(I'm a) Soldier in the Army of the Lord"
Performed by Lyle Lovett

"Shine On"
Written by Dolly Parton
Performed by Dolly Parton

Ruby Terry appears Courtesy of Malaco Records
Billy Joe Shaver appears Courtesy of Justice Records

Soundtrack Album Available on RISING TIDE RECORDS

Filmed with Panavision® Cameras and Lenses

Lighting Equipment Provided by Victor Duncan

Grip Equipment Provided by
Paramount Production Support, Inc.

Shot on Eastman Kodak Film

Color by CFI

SPECIAL THANKS
Walter Murch
Lafayette Convention & Visitors Commission
Cross Circle J Ranch, Inc.
Houma-Terrebone Tourist Commission
Kerry & Sharon Boutte
Louisiana State Film Commission
KVOL
Texas State Film Commission
KPEL
Terrebonne Parish President Walter Comeaux
Delhomme Funeral Homes
Terrebonne Parish Sheriff Donald J. Breaux
Tropical Fish Bowl
Trailways National Bus System
Royal Doulton
Sazerak Company, Inc.
H&H Lures
Wild Turkey
E.M.I.
Delta Media Corporation
97.3 The Dawg
Lee Clardy
Michael Dyckman
Michelle Archer
Rob McEntegart
Tim Metcalf of Deano's Pizza
Dickies, Inc.
Red Kap, Inc.
Friema Grylack at New Act Travel, Inc.
Michael McNamara

Countess Mar
Gerard Sellars
Joel Jacobson and Provident Financial Management
Irwin Tenenbaum and Sinclair, Tenenbaum,
Emanuel & Fleer
and
Sister Jewell Jernigan

In memory of
Reverend Isham Williams

With Gratitude and Thanks to
Helen Williams

The persons and events in this motion picture are fictitious.
Any similarity to actual persons or events is unintentional.

This motion picture is protected under laws of
the United States and other countries. Unauthorized
duplication, distribution or exhibition may result
in civil liability and criminal prosecution.